Also by Tom French

Riverviews: A History of the 1000 Islands in 3-D

WIND
WATER
WAVES

To Mark,
For helping me help the kids make their own ...

RIVER STORIES
BY TOM FRENCH

Tom

STONE ISLAND PRESS
POTSDAM, NY

The Last of the Old Timers and *Mom Makes River a Garden* previously appeared in *Thousand Island Life.*

Cover Photo Courtesy of Jon Taylor

For Gramp

Contents

The Last of the Old Timers

Jake yanked on the front door, felt the brief suction, then pushed the clanky storm. It rattled as a rush of cool air blew in.

"You're not going down there alone." Emily hobbled from the kitchen. "Wait until Bobby gets back."

"I'm getting antsy. I'm going to walk down. When they get back, send Bobby. He knows the way."

"Now, don't you do any of that work by yourself. I don't want you pulling that boat all alone. Chase your work and your work will chase you! You just sit there and wait for Bobby."

Jake frowned. "Don't you worry, dear." He pressed the flimsy aluminum storm door to make sure it was shut, then tacked a note for Bobby, his grandson, on the outside trim. Emily would never remember where he'd gone.

1

The air was crisp and bit his cheeks, though the rest of his body was warm under several layers of clothes. He ambled down the sidewalk and immediately realized he should have brought his cane. He hated to use it. In his mind he could still convince himself he was only in his thirties or forties. Yet when he glanced in a mirror, or at his hands, he knew. He remembered his father's hands — big, strong, textured. Strangely, he couldn't recall his hands ever looking like his father's. His hands were always young hands and then they were old — wrinkled, translucent, blotchy, dry, and fragile.

He took a shortcut through a field to the crest of Patterson's Hill where he had a commanding view over the tops of several houses to South Bay glimmering through the leafless trees.

He plodded down the hill out of the grass, crispy from frost, past Crystal Bay, and onto the small peninsula to his boathouse. He forced the rusty hinges and entered. The decking creaked under his feet. He swiped cobwebs away, brushing them from his face, and waited for his eyes to adjust to the dimness.

Two boats needed to be pulled — an old Starcraft bowrider and the fourteen-foot kicker. The Starcraft drifted in the slip. He was tempted to take it for one last ride. The river was calm, but he'd already been out for the last ride. He crouched, steadied himself with one hand on a post, and eased himself down, feeling the pleasant bob of the boat. He pumped the gas bulb a few times then slumped into the driver's seat.

He lifted the cold start, choked the motor, and turned the key. The starter whined. He kept pushing the choke and boosting the cold start until the engine roared into shrilling revolutions. He tapped the cold start down. The engine hummed softly; the water around the lower unit seethed and bubbled.

He went to the stern and detached the gas line from the motor, then returned to the driver's seat and waited for the gas to run itself through. It would be a few minutes. In the past he'd tried to speed

2

the process by putting the engine in gear — the lines taut and tugging on the cleats, the water behind the boat churning in the forced current, but it still took awhile and today he wasn't in a hurry.

He gazed into the brightness beyond the boathouse doors — across the water and bay and into the deep blue sky — blue as it had been for an eternity, allowing him to sometimes believe he could live forever. He scanned the opposite shore — the gray elms and oaks. He still saw things he'd never noticed before, even at this age, though they'd been in front of him his entire life. The speckled forest floor popped out at him. Deep in the bay the tall marsh grass had faded to the color of sand. He spotted a flock of ducks floating close to Harvey's Island and then four whistlers flew past heading into the bay.

He wondered how many more years, how many more autumns, if any, he would witness this hibernation. He loved the river. He did not doubt that. It was a part of his spirit and soul, and yet, he couldn't live with all its seasons and moods. His love was conditional. Part of him actually felt guilty for his defection. If he were a real man, he'd still grin and bear it as he had for years.

Then why not now when he no longer faced its rigors directly every day?

The walk had to be shoveled and the drafts could never be plugged and having to go for groceries or the mail or any number of other errands in the bitter cold. He shivered at the thought of it. Just being cooped up in the house all winter nettled him.

And the river was not without guilt either. He riveted his eyes on the spot in the bay where he'd last seen his first-born son — over a half century ago. A half century. There was no turning back.

It was a hard morning. This chore of pulling the boats would have been easier if the day had been mean and nasty. It was as if the river played with him, taunted him. As if it knew about the pressures his children were placing on him not to go to Florida because of their fears that he or Emily might fail while in Florida and be unable to return North, that he or Emily might become a burden if they were stuck in Florida so far away from the family.

"Let's face it, Dad. Your health is failing," Russell had said. Failing — the word rolled over and over in his mind. "And Mom's mind is going. If you end up in a hospital down there, who is going to take care of her? She's likely to set the house on fire or something."

He heard a flock of geese. It was a glorious morning and easy to forget the hard days and times this river had brought him. The mind was good at that — at forgetting the worst, even making it appealing in a sentimental way, but the years of experience had hardened him. He was too wise to be fooled by this conspiracy between his mind and the river.

The engine throbbed as it coughed for gas. It shook him from his thoughts. He swung around and revved the throttle, striving to keep the motor running for as long as possible, to make sure all the gas was burned and the engine was bone dry. It sputtered a few seconds longer, then died. He untied the four bumpers and heaved them on the dock.

"I thought I heard someone down here. Aren'tcha gone yet?"

Jake peeked up to see Wade's silhouette framed in the doorway. "Wade! Aren't you a sight for sore eyes." He stepped into the bow.

"It's a little late for ya this year, isn' it?" Wade spoke slowly.

"No, not really."

"When do ya leave?"

"Tuesday."

"Not 'til then?"

"Well, our flight leaves Tuesday morning. Russell will drive us to Syracuse on Monday." Jake reached up for the chain fall and pulled the hook. The chain links rattled through the pulley. He

4

leaned out over the bow and slipped the hook into the eye in the stem.

"Do ya remember liftin' ol' man Robinson's boat that one fall when the jacks broke?" Wade asked.

Jake observed Wade with a puzzled look. "No, I don't." It scared Jake because something inside him told him he should remember.

"You don'?" Wade seemed surprised. "Four of us there were — I was sure one of 'em was you. Are ya sure you weren' there?"

"Positive, Wade."

"Oh, well. The steel threads on the jacks had worn, and the cruiser was too heavy for the two beams and the screws, an' the cruiser collapsed an' fell right into the river."

"Whatcha you do when it fell in?"

"You should know, Jake. You were there."

"I'm tellin' you, Wade. I don't recollect being there. I sort of recall hearing about Robinson's yacht falling in," he lied. He didn't remember any of it. "But I wasn't there."

"Well, we borrowed a heavy fall from Hutchinson Boat Works an' two more from Doc Wilder. The water was low and we started hauling on the back an' we got her level and that's the way we brought her out — lifted her right up."

"Was that thirty-three or so?"

"Thirty-five."

"Wade, do you think you could hand me that strap?" Jake pointed to the rear wall where a wide canvas boat strap hung from a large spike driven into one of the studs.

"Sure, Jake." Wade ambled to the heavy strap, hoisted it off its hook, and handed the metal ends to Jake.

"Hey, Gramp." Bobby chuckled in the doorway. "It's a good thing I found your note. Grandma thought you'd gone to Clayton to trade horses."

Jake smiled as he tied a line to the metal rings on each end of the strap.

"Hello, son," Wade said. "Here to help your grandpa?"

"Yes, sir."

"Here, Bobby. Step down here in the boat. How strong are you feeling today?" Jake dropped the strap into the water and fished it around the engine and under the boat.

"As strong as ever."

"Good." Jake hooked the strap to the stern falls — one on each side of the boat. "I want you to pull on that chain, slowly, when I tell you." He pointed toward the bow. "But be prepared to stop. I've got two to pull and I might have to catch up occasionally."

Someone clamored outside on the gangway to the boathouse, then mumbled before appearing in the door.

"Why, Merle?" Wade said. "How are ya doin'? I haven't seen you in a while."

"I-I-I'm doing f-fine." He stuttered and swayed in the doorway.

"How'dcha know we were here?"

"I saw your truck, Wade. And I followed the kid down."

"Looking for a little action, are ya Merle?" Jake said. "Ready, Bobby?"

"Time t-t-to pull the boats, huh?" Merle slurred.

"Sure is. Got to head south."

Merle stumbled across the back of the boathouse to an old chest.

"Don't fall down now, Merle."

"Don't you worry, Wade. I've got my dock feet."

"Sea legs," Jake corrected.

"That too." Merle plopped down.

"Do ya remember the time we caught that sturgeon for the initiation of the Admirals, Merle?" Wade spoke louder over the babble of chains.

"I s-sure do, Wade. W-why do you ask?" Merle tottered on his seat.

"Well, your staggering around here reminded me of the initiation, that's all," Wade grinned.

"What's a sturgeon, Gramp?"

"Jus' one of the b-biggest fish you'll ever see," Merle said.

"How come we never fish for 'em then?"

"'Cause they're not in the river anymore." Jake tugged a length of chain. "Keep pullin' there, Bobby."

"Why not?"

"I'll tell ya why," Wade said. "The seaway and the moss that ya see on the rocks around on the bottom ruined the sturgeon. The sturgeon was a bottom feeder. And when the seaway stirred up the bottom of the river, we started noticin' this moss gettin' on the hooks an' when that started, that ended the sturgeon. They starved to death."

The boat began to swing from side to side and water dripped underneath. "Now watch out, Bobby. We're comin' out of the water. The boat's going to rock and it'll be harder to pull since we're liftin' the full weight now." He yanked another length of chain through one pulley and then the other.

"Did you ever catch a sturgeon, Gramp?"

"Sure did, but not as many as Wade."

"Oh, it was a nasty business," Wade said. "'Course, we were younger then."

"You ain't kiddin'," Jake agreed.

"Amen to that," Merle said.

"Ya had to grapple the line up an' start tying the damn bait on the hooks." Wade mimicked the movement. "A piece a cut up perch, in cold water, an' I wanna tell ya, I done it so many times my hands'd be numb an' sometimes your stomach would ache from the cold. But Jesus, they jus' cried for those fish. They'd call us up from New York on the phone, person-to-person, to ship

7

'em down, they wanted 'em so bad. An' we were gettin' two dollars an' forty cents a pound for 'em — hog dress'd! At that time, that was a lot of money!

"We'd cut the heads off an' take the innards out an' put the fish in a wooden barrel, which ya don't see nowadays, an' fill it full of ice, an' put the cover on, an' seal it around, an' take it off to the railhead, an' ship it down to this Van Shinton an' Company down in that Fulton Fish Market in New York City, an' they'd ship the check right back to us. Some time the check was a hundred and forty, fifty dollars!"

"Tell 'em ab-bout Booty and Buck," Merle said.

"Oh, I've had my run-ins with them too," Jake sighed.

"Yeah, well, we kept a boat, a flat-bottomed boat, in Horse Bay, and one time, Merle an' I went down to set the line an' there was somebody ahead of us there — Booty Joiner and Buck Calhoun. They were out in a skiff an' we stopped to say hello to 'em an' they had this thirty-thirty rifle sittin' on their seat with the damn thing cocked, an' they kinda nodded their heads as though 'get the hell outta there or they'd blast our heads off,' an' we left there that time an' didn't set our line."

Bobby gaped at Wade. "Do you think they would have shot you?"

"Oh, I don't think so. They were jus' strange people. Liked to keep to themselves."

"D-damn strange," Merle spat.

"Twisted, if you ask me," Jake said.

"Well, a week or so later we went down there an' there was nobody around, and so we set our line and started catchin' sturgeon immediately. On the first night we had two fairly good sturgeon, an' man those things were big. Fact, one of 'em was seventy pounds. What a thrill it was when ya had one on. Ya threw a grapple over an' ya grappled the line up, an' the minute ya got the line up, ya could tell if ya had a big fish on.

"We pulled 'em in an' ya could see 'em comin'. Usually they were pretty tired 'cause they'd been on quite a while, but ya still had to get these monsters into the boat. Now when ya see a sixty, seventy-five, or a hundred pound sturgeon, mister," he fixed his eyes on Bobby, "underwater — you've seen a fish. An' the biggest one I ever seen was a two-hundred pounder.

Bobby stared wide-eyed at Wade.

"Keep pullin' that chain," Jake said.

"What we would do, as one got near the boat, is we would gaff him. Now, ya couldn't gaff him in the stomach, 'cause ya had to keep him alive and they'd die quickly if ya weren't careful. An' if they were dead, ya couldn't ship 'em to New York. Ya had to have 'em fresh. So what we had to do was to get 'em jus' right, get 'em jus' under the mouth or behind the gill an' get him into the boat. An' then we threw life preservers an' bags or anything we could get over the damn fish. They'd pound so on the bottom of the boat we were afraid it'd sink us! An' we'd hike right for shore, immediately, quit everything, an' get 'em in the fish cage before he died. An' that was the whole secret of keepin' the fish alive."

Gravel crunched outside.

"Who's here now?" Merle asked.

Wade peeked out the door. "Why, it's Bennie."

"P-pulling these b-boats is turning into a regular t-town meetin'," Merle slurred.

"Yes, but I haven't seen any help from you fellows yet." Jake observed Bobby. "Slow down there, now, Kid. I need to catch up." Jake continued rolling the chains through the pulleys.

Bennie's feet scuffed on the dock outside as he appeared in the doorway. "Why it's a goddamned party and no one invited me."

"How d-did you know?" Merle stammered.

"I followed your breath down here. What have we got going here anyway?"

"Well, Gramp and I are pulling the boat. Wade is telling

stories, and Merle's just sittin' around."

The men howled.

"Damn kid."

"Well, some things never change," Bennie said.

"Bennie, maybe you and Wade could put those beams underneath." Jake pointed to the side of the boathouse.

"Sure thing, Jake. Why don't you get the other end there, Wade?" Bennie slid one end of an old gray cedar six-by-six from the side of the boathouse wall and dragged it to the opposite side of the boathouse so it lay across the slip.

"This is the p-problem with big b-boats," Merle said. "I can p-pull my jon boat all b-by my-s-self."

"Ya still have that thing?" Wade asked as they skidded the timber under the stern.

"You're lucky it doesn't sink and drown ya," Jake jeered.

Bennie and Wade positioned the second beam under the bow.

"Why, remember that old sharpie, Jake?" Bennie asked.

"I remember losing it." He plodded to the bow — the boat rocking beneath him.

"Watch out, Gramp."

"Don't you worry, Bobby. It's not going anywhere." He took the chain from his grandson and rocked the boat on purpose. "Now we use this other chain here and you just lift it up and the chain fall will take it and lower the boat." The chain rattled; the boat sank. "Got it?"

"Uh-huh."

Jake shuffled to the stern and grasped the chains. "Okay, now, very slowly, feed the chain up into the pulley and we'll lower her down onto the beams."

The chain chattered as the boat sank and swayed.

"How'dcha lose a boat?" Merle asked.

"You tell 'em, Bennie. I might be biased in my opinions of some people in the story."

10

"Well, one winter Jake and I built two sharpies. One apiece for each other."

"What's a sharpie?" Bobby asked.

"It's a boat," Jake said. "Pointed on one end and square on the other, flat-bottomed, used for trappin' and huntin' and fishin'."

"B-boarded c-crossways, ins-stead of lengthways," Merle added.

"Yeah, well," Bennie continued. "We always opened the season in Delaney's Bay, which was owned by Booty Joiner on one side and Buck Calhoun on the other. Now, we both built blinds on our sharpies so we could hunt separately and we were on Mosquito Island and the wind was coming up in the evening and Jake said, 'It looks like it might blow a gale. I think I'll take my blind up tonight.' You know, tow it up with the other boat. 'Then it'll be all set in the morning. How about you?' And I said 'Well, I'm not going up there in no gale wind.' So he took his boat up there and the next morning he routed right out about four-thirty or five and took off. I didn't go 'cause the wind was blowing pretty hard and I never was as big a daredevil as he. But about an hour later he come back. And I said, 'whatcha doin' back here?' Well, his sharpie, with the blind and all, was gone. When he went back, there was nothing there. He didn't have no blind to hunt out of — nothin'. So we monkeyed around. I run up there with 'em and naturally we ran right into Buck Calhoun and that other character, Booty Joiner."

"Yeah, we've already heard about them today," Jake interrupted.

"That's right," Bennie continued. "And 'oh, they hadn't seen any boat' or anything."

"Of course not," Jake mumbled.

"Yeah, and the huntin' was all over by then. So Buck, he gets in his boat and goes out and helps us look around."

"Hell, he was part of the deal!" Jake shouted. "He and that

11

Booty sunk that boat! They took her out in the Canadian channel and filled her full of rocks to keep us guys out of there and she lays out there in the middle somewhere to this day."

"They fixed ol' Jake here good. See, they'd started postin' that marsh, which is illegal. We figured it was illegal anyway. We didn't pay no mind to those posters. But we never did go back there, did we Jake?"

"Nope. No sense foolin' around with characters like that, but I'm not the only here whose lost a boat. Remember that time we were huntin' together with Dexter Hewitt on Mosquito?" Jake reminded Bennie. "The ducks were sittin' down there, raftin', and we decided you should go down and make a little circle?"

"That's illegal!" Wade said.

"Of c-course it is!" Merle yelled, almost falling off his seat.

"Don't tell me you never did anything illegal, Wade," Bennie said.

"Never."

"Aw," they all admonished him.

"Now let me finish my story. Bennie here, he started out with my sharpie. This was before it was gone, with a little five-horse — brand new five-horse too. And when he gets down there, there was a little followin' sea. Not a big wind or anything, just a followin' sea. Hewitt says, 'Bennie's driftin' down there.' And I says, 'he is?' 'Yeah, looks to me like he's waving — way down by Flat Iron.' 'Well, he must be in trouble.' So I got in the other boat and rushed right down there, and there he was, and he didn't have any motor. The clamps had loosened and he set there kind of half numb with his hand on the handle. One of them followin' seas had licked it and lifted it right up and took it right out of his hand. Brand new motor!!"

They all roared.

"Yeah, yeah. It's true, but at least it was your motor," Bennie gibed. "Either way you look at it, you lost both your boat and your motor."

"Not by my own doin' in either case, but do you think that's the end of that story? No way. In May of the next spring, along comes Coot Mulhull. He says, 'I've got somethin' Jake; it belongs to you.' I says, 'You have?' 'Yeah, it's right here in the back of my pickup.' I says, 'What is it?' 'Five-horse Johnson.' And there she was. I said, 'Where'd ja get that?' 'Well,' he says, 'I was on Flat Iron that day when it fell off. I saw Bennie and I put a range on that motor, where it was, and I went out there this spring...' on that range that he had across from one side to the other. And he looked down in the clear water and there laid the motor. He said, 'Jake, I'll sell ya the motor.' And I said, "Coot, I'll tell you something right now. I'm givin' you that motor. You found it, you can have it."

"Did it work? Did it work?" Bobby asked.

"Hell, no. All them cylinders'd be rusted and seized. It'd been laying in the St. Lawrence River all winter. Never get that motor runnin'. After six months? Nice of him to bring it back though, wasn't it?"

"Sure was."

Jake smiled at his grandson. The chain slackened as the boat rested on the beams. "That's it, Bobby. Bennie, stick those blocks under the stern, would ya?"

Bobby vaulted to the dock. As his feet thumped on the deck, a loud crash rang out from the back of the boathouse. Jake peered over the bow. Merle lay on the floor in a pile of lines and fishing poles that had fallen on him as he fell off the bench. He struggled to untangle himself. "Are you okay, Merle?"

"Yes, I'm f-fine. It's j-just this d-damn chest! It s-slipped out from u-under me."

Everyone hooted.

"You don't think it was you or the booze now, do you, Merle?" Bennie teased.

13

"Of c-course not. I've only had th-three drinks t-today."

"Big ones," Bennie laughed.

Merle stood. "Well, I-I'm not going to s-stick around here and b-be made f-fun of."

"Aw, now, Merle. No hard feelings," Wade said.

"I'll s-see you all l-later." Merle stumbled out.

Jake clambered over the gunnel to the dock.

"It's about lunch time," Bennie said. "I think I'll be going too."

"Yes, I believe it is," Wade said. "I should be goin' myself. If I don't see ya again, Jake, have a good winter."

"I will, Wade. You do the same."

"I'm sure I'll see you before you go." Bennie strayed toward the door.

Jake waved. "I'm sure too."

They disappeared outside off the dock.

"Is that all Gramp? I'm hungry too."

"Almost. We still have the kicker."

"Oh, yeah."

"Tell you what. Why don't you go out to the kicker? We'll get her going and you can take out all the bumpers and cushions while the motor drains its gas and I finish with this one. I just have to lube it."

"Okay." Bobby dashed out to the side of the boathouse.

Jake followed. It took several pulls to start the motor and Jake suddenly felt nauseous and tired. He popped off the gas line. "Now, Bobby, when this thing starts to sputter, I want you to rush back here and keep twisting the throttle until the engine stops. Do you understand?"

"Yeah, I remember doing this last year with you."

"Good." Jake struggled out and returned inside. He was hot, sweating profusely, and felt like he was going to faint. He sat on the dock and leaned against the wall.

14

"All ready, Gramp." Bobby came into the boathouse. "What now?"

Jake glimpsed Bobby, breathed deeply, labored to keep his grandson and the question in focus. He was exhausted. "We'll have... your father... come down here... and drag it out... for us."

Sweat stung his eyes and poured off his forehead. He wiped it off with the sleeve of his shirt. He squinted and blinked. He inhaled then exhaled deeply, keeping his head low, bent over. Suddenly his chest felt tight — like it was going to explode. He gripped his shirt and moaned. "Ahhh." He grimaced and his body coiled.

"Gramp! Are you okay?"

"Yeah," he forced.

"Are you sure? I'm going to go get some help." Bobby whirled abruptly.

"No!" Jake barked. Bobby stopped and looked back at him. "It's just... bad heartburn," Jake stammered. "It happens...... all the time." The pain began to pass. He fumbled in his pocket for his nitroglycerine, concentrated on his breathing — deep, steady, forceful breaths. He looked at his grandson and perked up.

"Geez, Gramp. You really scared me there for a minute. I thought you were having a heart attack or something."

"No. Just Grandma's... cooking." Jake made circles with his index finger on the side of his head.

Bobby laughed. Jake chuckled too. Then Bobby lowered his head and scuffed the dock with his sneakers. "Do you ever worry about dying, Gramp?"

"It happens... to all of us." He was still having difficulty.

"Yeah, I know, but does it scare you? It scares me sometimes."

Jake pursed his lips, heaved another deep breath. "Oh,...... I don't know. Sometimes. But it...... scared me more...... when I was young,...... like you. Now? Well......" His voice drifted off.

15

He knew it was another heart attack. It wasn't the first time — though this had been the worst. He'd hidden the attacks from Emily and the family because he knew the big one, the last, was close at hand. He knew if anyone suspected, they'd insist he go to the hospital. That would mean tests. He'd miss his flight or they wouldn't let him go at all. The collusion between his children and Emily and the doctor was something he couldn't fight.

He gazed away from Bobby toward the marsh, deep into the bay, at the golden reeds and then above the cattails, through the bare trees rising behind the river — into the heart of the forest and gilded leaf-covered floor. If he was going to die, he wished he could do it here. It would almost be pleasant to lie on the forest bed, enjoy the serenity of the sky through the trees with a warm, soft breeze off the river, and then close his eyes — to rest. He would rather die at the river — but not in the cold. "I'm just so tired." He said it more to himself than to Bobby. He took a deep breath and sighed.

"Should we go, Gramp? I'm awfully hungry."

"Just a few more seconds, Bobby. I want to enjoy this view… just a little bit longer. It might be the last time…… I'm down here…… this year." But Jake knew it might be the last time in his life. He'd seen this bay thousands of times — in all seasons and weathers and years. In an instant he tried to remember them all as they merged into a few brief memories. It had come to this — a perfect day. He stared across the water — the dark blue under the light blue, the sand-colored marsh, the specks of ducks in the bay, the light so bright it cried for him to stay.

But then the wind shifted to the north — just a light gust. It nipped his face and arms — drying the sweat. Tiny ripples on the water formed a small cat's-paw that sparkled speckles of yellow light. Soon it would be a gale and Jake knew the day was just a ruse, a trick — and he wouldn't be fooled. He was too old to start spending his winters here again. As much as he loved the river, it was the spring and summer and early fall that he loved. He stood, taking one last view of the bay, engraving it in his memory so he would never forget, no matter what.

Small River Running Wide

It's late and the air is thick and sultry, even by the river. A waning moon slips gently in and out of luminescent clouds. Its white light shimmers and bounces between the ripples of a cat's-paw. A faint halo encircles the moon – late notice of an approaching storm. In the distance, lightning flashes behind the towering clouds of the front — lurid and foreboding. It has been a rainy summer.

Two boats float silently in their slips. Your feet rest on the stern fiberglass hull of one. It bobs beneath your heels. A string of boats tied together, like the tail of a kite, drift downriver from the dock. Until recently, only Blair would dare do that, even when there was docking space.

Voices seep out of the upstairs boathouse apartment. Some sing and dance along to Eric. Their feet pound on the floor, drumming with the rumble of the distant thunder, their voices out of tune. Eric's been playing his guitar for hours, but he hasn't repeated a single song. It's amazing he can play so many songs and know all the words. Someone is shaking the big red plastic piggy bank filled with pennies like a maraca. Blair used to do that too.

Eric stares over as you walk back inside. His gaze is trancelike. He concentrates on playing, yet he never glances at his guitar. His face is covered with the dark rubble of a young beard. He hasn't shaved for weeks. He's never looked like this before. Blair had a beard. It was long and unkempt and fluffy and red.

Andy, Claire, and Mark sit on the couch browsing through some photo albums. You sit on the arm of the couch and look over Claire's shoulder.

"Look at this one." She flips the stiff pages, throwing her long blonde hair as she does. "This one is real good, don't you think?"

"Yeah," you say. "It's neat. I wouldn't mind a copy of that one." It's a picture of Blair standing at the helm of his 17-foot whaler taken from behind and twenty yards away. The bow is high out of the water. The stern and 95-horse Johnson are low and surging down so the boat appears to be standing up vertically out of the water — an instant before it planes off. The sun is directly in front of him, close to setting, so Blair and his boat are just a silhouette.

The day Blair died is still clear — it was only seven weeks ago. It could just as easily have been you. It could have been you. You've even thought more than once it should have been.

It was a Saturday and it was sunny. The blue sky encased you in this world with only the river and the islands and Blair and you in your boats. He was your wingman. He buzzed up to your port

20

side, splashing water over the gunnel as he threatened to charge ahead, rejoicing merrily with his beard and long hair waving in the wind. It was foolish. It was dangerous. You knew this. But it was fun and Blair went along. You didn't think twice about it — never did when Blair was around. You just did it.

But then he fell into formation aft, letting you take the lead though your small tin boat was the slower.

A large flock of ducks had landed between Murray and Grenell. They packed the water down the length of the two islands – dozens of them. You steered straight for the center of the flock. They were whistlers.

The ones closest jumped first. Then the ones in front — more and more stretching their wings like a wave lifting off the water always a hundred yards off your bow. Soon the sky was so full, the ducks were like a cloud blocking the sun — their feathers flashing black and white to the quick beat of their wings. They circled with suspicious eyes, waiting for you to leave. And still there were more.

Suddenly, a small flock of seven geese lifted from within the wave. They were much bigger than the whistlers and more graceful with their large wingspans. They moved in slow motion. They followed a leader. They didn't break up. They stuck together. Blair slowed to a stop to watch the ducks and geese circle. You pulled up to his gunnel and drifted into his side. He wore reflective sunglasses and when you looked at him, you saw yourself.

After dinner, the two of you hooked up with his brother, Miles, and went to the Pub. You stayed too long, drank too much — a continuation of the day.

Outside, a fog had slipped in, and when you walked to the dock, a ship was blowing its horn.

You untied your boat. Blair fiddled with his running lights while Miles untied their boat, then they drove away and

21

disappeared into the fog. The stern light was the last thing you saw. Your stomach was tight, uneasy because of the fog, but you started your engine and drove off toward the narrows.

The lights on the foot of Murray were bright enough to guide you to the gut, but it was spooky the way the wind blew. It was usually calm in a fog. The backside of Murray was dark except for one light. You pointed the bow across Eel Bay and took a heading using the light – seven o'clock on the stern. The silhouette of Murray vanished quickly but the light was still clear.

You kept searching for a light from Grandview. There had to be at least one. The yellowing light on Murray began to fade. You could have doubled back and spent the night at Eric's but decided to try for home. The light on Murray evaporated. You kept the boat straight by watching your wake. The boat bounced on the waves — one... two... three... four... five... six... seven. One... two... three... four... five... six... — every seventh wave the biggest. But still no sign of land — thirty seconds, a minute, maybe two. Surely Grandview should have been in sight by now.

It would be futile to turn around with no way of knowing which was the correct way. The wind was out of the east at the dock. But that wouldn't help either. Wind and waves twist and distort around the islands. You didn't know the river well enough to know its winds. You slowed the boat and killed the engine. People had done complete circles in a fog. Shoals littered Eel Bay. It was better to drift and wait for the fog to rise.

You lay down. It felt like the boat was spinning wildly. It was dizzying, but it was only the wind and fog and booze. You fell into a light sleep, a fine mist caressing your face.

When you awoke, the fog had lifted. The boat was drifting near shore. At first you thought you had floated into Canada, but it was only the foot of the bay. You cranked your engine and went home.

It's beginning to rain and it's pounding on the roof. The distant thunder rumbles closer. Lightning flashes outside. The lamps in the house answer with flickers. The windows rattle. The thunder and lightning is almost simultaneous. Everyone chants "Oouu." It's the first big close one.

"Play *Island Sunset*, Eric."

"Yeah, Eric. Play *Island Sunset*."

People chant "*Sunset*" loudly. "*Sunset, Sunset.*" Eric adjusts his harmonica holder. The chanting continues until he strums the first chord. He puts his mouth to his harmonica. It is a waltz – an island anthem. Everyone forms a circle around him. You squeeze between Claire and Mark, wrapping your arms into theirs, pitching and rolling in time as Eric starts the chorus. Everyone joins in.

> *There's nothing quite like an island sunset in the*
> *summertime with the wind blowing in off the*
> *waves.*
> *And I will always remember an isle sunset in the*
> *winter, when I am far away.*

During the verse, the swaying is slower and more prolonged. Eric's tenor voice is full and strong.

> *Sparkling light on the water as the wind dies down*
> *and friends gather 'round to sing a song or*
> *two.*
> *Laughter on the water as the sun goes down and I*
> *look and I see all my good friends are here*
> *next to me.*

Someone lets out a long high shout, "wooeeee," as Eric goes into the chorus again and everyone joins in.

'Cause there's nothing quite like an island sunset in
   the summertime with the wind blowing in off
   the waves.
And I will always remember an isle sunset in the
   winter, when I am far away.

Then only silence except for Eric's guitar and harmonica. He keeps time with the thunder outside. It sends a chill up your spine. Your eyes close as he enters the last verse. His voice is quiet. He picks his guitar softly.

Darkness on the water as the stars fill the night,
I'm as high as a kite and I never want to come down
'Cause my friends are around me and the islands
   surround me.
This is where I'll always hope to be.

He sings the chorus for the last time. Some sing along with him. A series of flashes illuminate the night and then long rumblings shake the house. The windows are steamed from the moisture and heat.

Summer is almost over. People start to leave, afraid the weather might get worse. You decide to leave too.

You don't go straight home though. You feel like being on the river even if it is raining. The boathouse disappears into the union of shoreline and trees and drizzle. It is a big river and you are but a speck in its wide expanse. The lights of a freighter move up the channel. You head out to buzz it. The rain collects in your hair and on your face as you pilot toward the open river.

You approach the freighter from behind. The turbulence from its wake shakes your small boat back and forth. You stay close to its stern for a few moments, only ten feet from its rudder. It dwarfs you and your boat. It looms above, black and large. It rumbles your whole inside – the only thing you can see.

You push the throttle arm quickly and sharply to the right. The engine cavitates briefly as the trough of your wake traverses through the prop. You speed forward, sliding along the ship's port side, matching its speed. The captain and his mates must think you're crazy to be out in the rain in the late night buzzing its side. Then again, maybe they don't even see you. You reach your hand out and run your fingers on the rough cold steel before accelerating, pulling ahead, and crossing its bow. A surge of water bubbles at its nose. You clear its path, stop, and watch it cruise away upriver — its lights blinking from the rain.

Swinging downriver you approach a green buoy and bear straight for it — challenging it. At the last moment you avoid it by pushing the throttle arm hard. The splash of water hits the metal as you head off for the next one. It's red. You buzz each one wide open — red, green, green, red. The rain recedes to a fine mist. It looks like fog. Soon it will be.

You turn your boat toward home after veering by one last buoy — a green one. The fog is thicker, but it doesn't seem strange being on the river at this hour, in this weather, at this time. Riding out of the narrows, you point the bow toward Grandview. You'll make it home tonight, no matter what happens. And you'll know this river too, even if it's the last thing you do.

Mom Makes River a Garden

I imagine Mom has a dream of making the river a garden from Clayton to Alexandria Bay, of covering the ten miles of shore with a thick jungle of flowering vines & creepers and filling the bays & channels between the countless islands with water lilies, blue flag, duckweed, and lily pads for frogs to sun on and birds to sing about. But she never gets further than her own dock — and even there she has trouble with the muskrats eating her flowers at night.

Japanese tourists stop because they think it's a public garden. Mom runs down to the dock to say it is private property and the

Japanese look at her strangely. They are only taking pictures. Gardens are sacred in Japan.

"Those Japanese," she mumbles as she walks back into the house. "Don't let them fool you. They understand more English than they let on."

Today, when Mom is on the dock with flowers in her arms, a Japanese man asks if she works there.

"Yes," she replies.

"Are those perennials?" The Japanese man points from his boat.

"No, they're zinnias." And she chuckles as she continues with her chores.

Mom starts her garden in early spring with a trip to Kingston. The Farmers' Market is on Thursdays. On a clear morning she leaves in her old dark-green Arkansas Traveler with the Johnson ten-horse. She doesn't believe in bigger or faster boats. It takes two hours to cross the river and go the twenty miles. She wears two sweaters and wraps a flowery red bandana around her graying hair. She goes by way of the Bateau Channel and, if it is calm, returns in late afternoon by crossing Forty Acres. I journeyed with her when I was small and she was younger. I rode in the bow of the boat. I held on to the bowline all the way, tight, as a rein, feeling the brunt of every wave like a cowboy on horseback.

It was always a spring day — cool and fresh with streams of freshly melted snow trickling down every pathway. Mom found a place to tie the boat close to shore on a large pier made for bigger boats. She knew it was safe because the water was so shallow so close to shore. We had to climb up out of the boat; the pier was that high. As we strolled to the market, the curbs steamed in the spring heat and I held her hand. We marched up Brock Street one block to the parking lot behind the Courthouse.

The vendors would be at their stalls — a table behind a car or truck. Some had makeshift awnings covering their tables, chairs, and wares. As we ambled between the rows, they would sit, or stand, and smile, and watch us — their faces filled with hope and anticipation that we would buy.

"Good day?"

"How are you?"

"Beautiful morning?"

Each statement inflected an uncertainty — their accents lifting off and hanging in the air, awaiting a reply, a confirmation. Their remarks not merely statements, but volleys.

Mom was meticulous. I watched her; she was never out of my sight. She studied the flowers, put her hands right into the green, pressed the soil and wrapped her fingers around the stems and leaves and buds. From stall to stall she wandered.

"They're the best peonies here."

"I can see that," and she moseyed on.

But I admired the other stuff — cakes and muffins, cookies and pies, bread, maple sugar and syrup, fruits, and large jars of thick golden honey, which I flipped upside down to watch the bubbles slowly flow. Mom gave me a dollar.

One stall had a tall vase filled with peacock feathers. They were shiny and rainbowish — changing color as I moved. That was what I bought — two at fifty cents each.

Mom bought a bag of fresh cheese curd and shared it with me. It squeaked between our teeth. Then Mom began to buy her garden. She traveled the route between the stalls again — buying petunias from one man, a crate of English ivy and vinca vine from a husband and wife. They were carefully placed in old beer-case boxes. I made the trips to the curb. Mom's plants piled up near the fire hydrant on the corner of Brock and King in Kingston — African violets; an evergreen; geraniums; an hibiscus; dark blue lobelia; yellow snap dragons; deep red paintbrush; purple, white, and yellow pansies and violas; sweet alyssum; a little rose tree; a rose bush.

29

When Mom finished, she flagged a taxi. She slipped the driver a bill as she explained we only needed to go one block. She pointed to all the flowers. The driver loaded them into the trunk and back seat.

"Wait!" Mom said when he lifted a six-pack of yarrow. "That needs to be in front where it will get light."

The taxi driver didn't even hesitate. When everything was loaded, we packed ourselves in and trekked to the boat — me in the middle with the plant needing light in my lap. The driver helped unload the flowers. He even carried them the short distance and set them on the pier above the old Arkansas Traveler. Mom climbed down and I handed her the boxes and she placed them carefully between and on the paint-chipped wooden seats.

Mom drove home carefully, throttling down for every wave and slowing whenever a pedal or leaf shook violently and looked like it might fall off and blow away. None ever did. I nestled in the bottom of the boat where the mauve rhododendron petals tickled my face as I made sure none of the boxes fell off their seats.

She started planting as soon as we were home. She dug out last year's roots from whatever she was planting in and placed peat moss in the hollow created. She used a sharp knife to cut the plants out of their containers. She'd put the plant in the dirt and pack the soil around it. She'd hum and have me fill the water bucket from the river to sprinkle her work.

"Keep going," she said.

"But it's drenched!"

"That's okay," her hands dirty and fondling the next plant. "They need a lot of water."

I poured and poured. I meandered to the edge of the dock and lowered the bucket in again and again. The water fingered, tendrilled, and sank into her soil.

Then the garden was planted. Soon it bloomed and bloomed

and bloomed. The vines snaked out into paths; the ivies dangled from their perches among the trees — down to the dock, along the shore, covering the yard, encircling the house, on the deck, and in the windows — pouring out of ceramic pots and vases. People slowed as they drove past. The Japanese stopped.

Mom prunes and waters daily. She tosses the snipped and broken buds into the river. They drift downstream in a steady line pointing the way for the Japanese like the bread in *Hansel and Gretel*. I watch the Japanese from the riverbank as they point into the water at the orange, red, and white begonia petals or the purple and pink petunias — their faces filled with awe and their mouths fluttering in their foreign tongue. They weave from flower to flower in their rented boats, kickers with nine-nines, stopping and staring at each bloom like it is its own garden.

Mom taught me to snip the old wilting flowers behind the buds, and I toss them into the river too.

Her favorite is the night blooming cereus and when it blooms she finds me and together we sneak down in the evening with a flashlight and peer into the folds of its huge ivory blossom. It has a magic scent. Like a fine perfume my mother wears it. She flaps and waves her hands to bring the sweet smell to her nose.

"Oh, do you smell that? Isn't that exquisite?" She whispers in my ear.

Yet in the fall the garden fades. The leaves dry and yellow and brown and crumble. The stems go limp or harden like ribbon candy until the day the garden's not there at all. I inhale the memories as a fragrance, though they are fading like a dream in the morning when you can't remember the night except for the bits and pieces. I scramble to collect each clipping to graft what the daylight has broken.

Just a Hint of Halloween

It was Mark's idea to have the séance. I was out cruising around the river, just messing around in the boat on an Indian summer evening, when I came out of the narrows into Eel Bay and saw Mark in his kicker tied alongside Eric's Hutchinson, drifting and watching the sunset. I turned toward them and sped across the loose chop.

"I'm so glad I ran into you," I shouted to Eric as I reversed my stern into his boat and lashed my line to a cleat on his gunnel. "I was just thinking about your Halloween party."

He glanced down at the river. "We're not going to have it this year."

"What?! Why not?" I asked. "It wouldn't be Halloween without your party."

"Claire said she wasn't up to it anymore and I agreed. It's a lot of work and it's gotten out of hand. People we never see all year come, drink our beer, make a mess of the place, and then leave without even saying 'thanks.' Besides, it just doesn't seem quite right after what happened to Blair."

Mark sat pensively on a cushion in the middle bench of his small kicker, leaning against the gunnel, legs up on the seat, facing the sunset, his dark ponytail swaying with the gentle rock of the boat. He leaned back further and his boat tipped more to one side. "I've got an idea that's better than any party, for just the three of us."

"Well, let's hear it," I said. "I'm all ears."

"Let's go up to Birnam and have a séance. Halloween's the perfect night to have one."

Eric shook like a shiver was being sent down his spine. "You know the stories about Birnam. That ghost just might come back and start talking."

As much as Eric was jesting, he was also right. Birnam Isle had always been known for ghosts and one in particular — Hamilton Beaumont. He'd been murdered there. There was even a story that Blair had been possessed for an entire night. His family had gone camping on the island and he and Miles, his brother, had climbed the tallest tree, a virgin pine — the one Hamilton Beaumont was supposedly hung from. When they finally came down, Blair took out all his change and keys from his pockets and ran around the island, stumbling in the leaves while mumbling about the governor and embezzling money — at least the story goes.

"Isn't that sort of the point?" Mark's voice reverberated on

34

the boats. "To commune with the dead?"

"All right, I'm in," Eric said. "I'll do it, but what about Miles and Mia? Should we invite them to go?"

I laughed. "Would you want to be invited to a séance that might call up your dead brother?"

"I might."

"This whole idea is nuts." I shivered too.

Mark peered at me with a twinkle in his dark eyes. "Yes, but are you with us?"

I surveyed the sunset and the islands. The western horizon blended into a burnt auburn with the trees. "I guess. I'd never do it alone, but with the bunch of us? Hell, what's the worst that could happen? It wouldn't be the first time someone saw spirits on Birnam."

So the three of us agreed to meet at the Main Dock at eight o'clock on Halloween — Eric, Mark, and myself.

I arrived first. I sat on the edge of the dock with my feet bobbing on the gunnel of my Starcraft, hypnotized by the stars shimmering on the river. I waited in the darkness, listening to the easy slap of water on the piers and shore, the cool crisp air biting my cheeks. In the distance, I heard the steady rudimental hum of Eric approaching in his Hutchinson, and a little louder to the left was the buzz of Mark's outboard — the only two boats on the river.

A small group of children passed on the road dressed in their costumes. I don't think they saw me, but then, it was a black night and I never saw the shadow behind me until after I was startled by a quick poke and my heart jumped. "Geez," I shrieked, but it was only Mia, Blair's sister. "You scared me," I said.

She was dressed warmly in charcoal-colored clothing and resembled a bandit in the night. "You deserve it for not including me in your plans."

"Sorry, but you seem to have found out."

"Mark told me."

"We were afraid it might upset you."

"Apologies accepted, but I'm always good for a little adventure. It's Miles who's freaked out."

The low inboard rumble of Eric's Hutchinson and the noisy discord of Mark's outboard approached and grew louder. They slowed to enter the small harbor. Eric glided the Hutchinson into the dock and drifted effortlessly to a stop. Right behind him was Mark twisting in his seat to reach back and throw his engine into reverse. His stern drew into the staving; the water foamed and churned around his prop. He tossed his lines onto the dock. "You guys ready?"

"As ever as I will be." I picked up Mark's bowline and tied it. He clambered out of his kicker and secured the stern.

Mia leaped into the Hutchinson. "Come on boys, let's go." She leaned against the windshield between the two front seats. "The witching hour will soon be here."

It was dark on the river, but Eric knew his way. The four of us stood behind the dash until we planed off — bow lights reflecting red and green on the water. Then we sat — except for Mia. She continued to stand in the aisle between Eric and me, her face above the glass staring into the wind, her Irish cheeks rosy, her red hair dancing off the nape of her neck, enchanted, like leaves blown from a tree. She was jubilant and she whooped into the night air. It was fall, though, so there was no one but us to hear her.

Eric didn't slow even as he approached the dock on Birnam. He swooped into the bay and pulled the throttle up at the last moment. The boat's wake washed forward under the hull as Mark and I sprang onto the dock with the lines. I'd never seen Eric dock like that before. It was something only Blair did.

"Bumpers out," he commanded as Captain. We tied the boat.

Eric took the lead. We followed him off the dock and up the rocky path toward the ruins through the ghostly forest. We felt our

36

way along with our feet. Leaves shuffled and billowed. I heard everyone's breathing and felt my heart pound.

The ruins were part of an old estate that had burned during the thirties. They were located on top of the single hill that made the island. Only the red granite foundation remained — ten feet high in places, but crumbling, especially where people had knocked it down. A simple maze that used to be the basement surrounded a wounded chimney — a tall monument to the past that still towered more than two stories. We reached the first outer wall and stopped to catch our breath.

"Let's go to the big room in front of the fireplace," Eric said.

"I think we should just leave and forget it," I suggested.

"Too late for the jitters." Eric withdrew into the maze. "I suppose you could wait in the boat," he called out.

"No backing down now," Mia said. "Just keep your head straight. The worst thing that could happen is Beaumont will show up and I've dealt with him before." She grinned at me.

I followed her through the opening toward the core of the ruins, over another pile of rubble and into the room at the base of the fireplace. It loomed above like an apparition with its big open hearth, wide and gaping five feet above our heads. We found the center of the room. Eric pulled a big round candle from his Army jacket. He lit it and placed it on the granite bedrock.

We sat around the candle on the rough, rocky, broken ground.

"Now, close your eyes and concentrate," Eric said. "Think about Blair. Call for *him*."

Mia shook her head. "Oh, *call for him*. Such hocus-pocus. Since when did you become a psychic?" She reached out and took my hand and we formed a circle.

We sat in the darkness for a few minutes, silently. My hands were sweaty — not because I believed, but because I was nervous it might actually work. We were trying to call the dead and it scared me. Every sound was amplified — the scratch of my nylon jacket on the rocks, the rumble of a ship in the channel, the screech of an owl. I heard a whisper and imagined it was the wind, but the river had been calm on the way over. Then I recognized it as the wash of water on the beach and was relieved until I pondered to myself, "That can't be. We're too far away from the beach to hear it up here." It got louder and I realized there had to be a wind for waves to be on the beach. Suddenly I heard the branches above swaying and clicking into each other.

I felt the hair on my neck lift and my heart race. The candle flickered, but not out, as the sudden windstorm swirled like a dust devil centered on us.

Something to the left caught my eye. As I turned my head slowly and slightly, I thought I spied a figure coming into the room. My eyes watered from the cold and it was hard to see in the darkness. I wanted to say something, scream in excitement and fear — but it was like a dream where you couldn't. I was frozen. Something held me. My whole body felt chilled.

I blinked and squinted — my brow creasing hard. The candle was so faint and everything was in shadows — the ruins, the trees, Eric, Mark, Mia.

For some reason I started thinking about Eric's Halloween party last year when Blair was voted best costume. He was a sailboat, or maybe he was just the mast. He had two sails on wooden dowels — one fore and one aft — cut from old t-shirts. He had to navigate carefully all evening.

Around us the wind whistled through the trees and over the ruins. It was from this wind that I heard Blair speak, slow and almost indiscernible, as he had at the party where he rolled among the crowd all night long saying, "Rough seas ahead. Don't follow me. Rough seas ahead" — his wooden dowels and sails flapping back and forth.

Then it was gone. The wind stopped. The candle went out. I heard Mia crying gently. Mark hugged her. "It's okay."

"I know," she said. "I just never believed. It was all a joke to me. But he was here. I felt him."

Mark helped Mia up and we strayed down the hill. Eric drove the boat slowly. No one said a thing. The motor hummed lightly. I gazed into the sky. I'd never seen so many stars and they all sparkled separate and distinct.

When we arrived at the Main Dock, Miles was waiting for us. "Well, what happened?"

"What do you think?" I answered. "Didn't you see anything?"

"How would I see anything here on the dock when you guys were up on Birnam?"

"Didn't the wind pick up or anything?" Eric asked.

"Sorry, I didn't notice," Miles quipped.

"Well, he was there, Miles," Mia sobbed.

"Sure. And what did he say?"

"He said 'Who put you in charge?'" Eric said.

"No he didn't," Mark murmured. "He said 'Nothing ever changes; nothing remains the same.'"

"I thought he said 'Play for keeps,'" Mia whispered.

Miles snickered even harder. "You guys should at least get your story straight. What did he say to you, Andy?"

I shook my head. "It doesn't matter. You wouldn't believe it." And I laughed. It's what Blair would have done. Eric, Mark, and Mia laughed too — laughing to the point of tears at what we'd seen and what we wanted to believe.

With the River and
In the Wind

I

First there was the river and then the wind running slow and silent and smooth — swirling mist against red granite streaked from lichen and flaring in the light of the fading sun and sparkling in the morning from the night's foggy haze. And in the frozen winters, the waters rippled and congealed and crystallized and the wind piled the snow near shore leaving the channel ice bare and flat and cold. The wind whistled through the pines and leafless trees clear and hollow — the breath of time's eternal song.

And then there was young Ben riding with Wild Jack across

the ice on the horse drawn sleigh — two white spotted mares only gray shadows through the storm. Wild Jack huddled, one hand on the reigns, the other on the neck of his scotch bottle, his hood pulled down low over his tight forehead and gray-blue eyes, whiskey frosted breath wrapping around his stubbly cheeks. Ben crouched next to him. He had been here before with the wind biting his face, seeping through his clothing into his small bones. The sleigh's skid marks quickly faded behind them in the wind and swirling snow until no path showed where they'd been — only the case of Wild Jack's liquor, the cans of kerosene, the bag of flour, and slabs of salt pork and other provisions, canvas covered in the sleigh's bed, to mark the journey's end.

"Why can't we go faster?" Ben asked even though he knew the answer. The sleigh crept forward much too slowly. The gray shadows of Bluff danced on the edge of his vision to the right.

"Don't want to overwork the horses in this cold. They'll get pneumonia for sure." Wild Jack took another swig of whiskey. At least it was only his first bottle, Ben thought. His father had sent him to make sure Wild Jack didn't get too drunk.

Ben hunched tighter into his coat and the blanket he had wrapped around himself. It had been clear that morning — the sky a faded blue with a dim and distant sun hollow and yellow and low on the frosted horizon. Not even any wind on the way to Clayton, only the sleigh's breeze on his face — cold, yet sweet. Now it was bitter and bit his cheeks. It had started to blow while they were in Cerow's Store — whistling through the door and rattling the windows. They were in a blizzard by the time they had the sleigh off Mary Street and on the ice, making their way home with only the direction of the wind to guide them — and a bottle of whiskey for Jack. It was all he needed he said.

"I'm cold."

"Here, have a taste of this. It'll warm you up." Wild Jack thrust the bottle into Ben's chest.

"I can't," Ben laughed. "Ma wouldn't approve."

"Ah, she'll never know. Drink it up. Don't you want to be a man?"

Ben took a small sip. It burned his mouth and throat.

"That was no sip. Take a good swallow." Wild Jack took the bottle, lifted it to Ben's mouth, and poured it in. Ben coughed and gagged and gulped. "There, that'll do you some good."

And then there was a crash — loud as thunder in front of them as the sleigh shuddered and the horses sank and disappeared from view.

"Jump! Quick!" Wild Jack yelled. He grabbed Ben by the collar and swung him around and out of the sleigh.

Ben's head spun as he flew through the air. The horses screamed over the wind and the ice roared in its thrashings. He rolled and tumbled onto the ice.

As soon as he could, he turned to look. The sleigh's skids stuck out over the broken ice, teetering on the edge, hanging precariously over the now open water. Wild Jack was cutting the reigns that tied the horses to the sleigh.

"Run for shore, Ben!" Wild Jack's voice seemed lost in the wind. Ben felt dizzy, but he ran, the shrieking horses and crashing ice blending into the wind behind him. He slipped and tripped and fell until he was suddenly knee deep in the shoreline drifts. In his panic, he hadn't even seen the trees, but now they loomed in front of him. He grabbed the ground and pushed himself to his feet, suddenly realizing that he was all alone and lost with no place to go. For all he knew, the sleigh and Wild Jack could have fallen through the ice too. He turned around and stared into the wind and snow, the whiteness blinding. Spots flashed in his eyes, but he had no choice. He started back onto the ice, marching into the storm, leaning forward with resolve.

The wind whipped about him. There was no sleigh, no islands, no river, no Wild Jack — only him and the wind and the ice and snow, but the sleigh, or its cold watery hole, was out there somewhere and he would find it no matter what.

And then he saw the fuzzy silhouette of Wild Jack in the corner of his eye — tall and wiry and bow-legged. The wind almost carrying him to shore like a giant sail.

"Jack!" Ben yelled. "Jack! Over here!"

Wild Jack stopped and cocked his head to the wind. "Ben!" They moved toward each other.

"I thought I told you to run for shore." The whiskey bottle still in his hand.

"I did, but when I got there, I didn't know what had happened to you and I had to find out."

"You should have stayed near shore. It's dangerous out here. The ice could be bad anywhere."

"But I'm light and small and you might have needed help."

Wild Jack took a swig of his whiskey. "Let's not argue about it now. There's an old abandoned cabin on Picton — part of the old quarry. I'll take you there and then go for help." He swung the bottle to his lips again. "Come on. Let's hurry. It'll be getting dark soon."

Ben followed Wild Jack across the ice, the wind pushing them as if telling them to leave. When they reached shore, he struggled behind Jack through the snow. Sometimes he sank up to his chest. Wild Jack would turn and lift him and help him along. They trudged, their legs kicking through the deep powder. The trees swayed, branches boxing each other — clicking, hooking, and creaking with each blow as the wind blasted every trunk with a vest of white.

The cabin was half buried in snow. A granite chimney towered above the roof on the north end and a pile of firewood was stacked along the side.

Wild Jack strode to the door, lifted the latch, and pushed. Wind and snow poured through like water from a flood as he and

44

Ben stumbled in.

Wild Jack looked around. "This isn't a bad shelter. At least it will keep you out of the storm."

"How long do we have to stay here?"

"*You're* going to stay here until I come back with help. I'll get a fire going. Help me bring in some wood." He turned around and Ben followed him back outside.

The woodpile was covered with snow. Along the edges, Ben could see the aging wood — dry and grey. The wind had blasted snow into every crack. He brushed the snow from a small section to reveal the top logs. He tried to lift one, but it was frozen in place. Jack snapped one off then used it to hammer the others loose.

"Here," Jack rapped two logs together to knock more snow off then cradled them in Ben's arms. He quickly stacked two more into Ben's arms. "Now go put those by the fireplace then come back for more."

Ben stumbled through the door with Jack right behind him. They made four trips. By the last one, a well-beaten path etched the ground to and along the pile, and small wood and bark chips littered the snow.

Jack dropped his last load onto the heap and said, "I'm going down to the sleigh to get some kerosene and matches. You wait here."

"But what if it fell in?"

"Then I'll use a little whiskey." He pulled the flask from his jacket, took a big swig, and grinned. "Don't you worry. I'll be back."

He slipped out the door. Ben stood on the threshold and watched him fade into the storm before he pushed the door closed.

He sat in a corner on the frozen dirt floor and waited. At first, he could feel the time, knew it had only been a few seconds and minutes, but then it all merged into the swirl of the storm and he didn't know how long it had been, whether time was standing still, moving slowly, or flying by. There was just the hiss and hum and moan of the wind and snow and sleet rolling over the eaves and rattling the glass of the windows. It could have been forever for all he knew.

And then the door flew open and Wild Jack pushed through, stomping his feet, and shaking the snow off his heavy coat, a can of kerosene in his right hand. "Whew," he slammed the door behind him with his elbow. "It's nasty out there." He walked over to the fireplace and set the kerosene down, then reached into his coat and pulled out a hunk of cheese and his flask. He tossed the cheese to Ben. "I thought you might be hungry."

Ben caught the cheese as Jack lifted the flask to his lips for a swill. Jack sighed as he swallowed, then shook the chill. "Whoof. Let's get a fire going." He pulled his gloves off, stacked three logs in the fireplace, and poured kerosene on top. He stood in front of the hearth as he flicked a match on the stone. The match head flickered in his palm. Once the flame was steady, he tossed it onto the wood and it spread along the surface of the logs — orange and arching and engulfing, hissing as the snow and ice melted and steamed away.

He knelt in front of the fire and warmed his hands on the growing flame. "I'm going to go for help and I want to get as far as I can before dark. You just stay here and keep this fire going. If it goes out, there's the kerosene and here are some matches." He set the box next to the pile of logs. "I'll be back as soon as I can."

And then Wild Jack stood, pulled on his gloves, and walked out, drawing the door shut behind him. Ben went to the window and watched him go — whiskey bottle in hand, disappearing into the wind and trees and snow, his figure distorted by the imperfections in the glass.

He sat on the cold ground in front of the fire and stared at the grayish black walls of the cabin and at the cloudy white of the snow swirling outside. Again, time had no meaning, no reference. He lay down, snuggled into his clothing and watched the flames dance. Hypnotized by their flickers and licks, he was soon asleep.

When he awoke, it was dark. At first he didn't know where he was — almost mistook it for a dream except the wind was too real and then he remembered the horses, the sleigh, and Wild Jack bringing him here. And in the darkness of the night, he felt the cold drafts of the wind seeping in through the cracks of the door and windows and every seam – the fire just a pile of glowing embers.

He sat up and reached for a log, tossed it into the fire, and then another and another and stoked it with a fourth. The flames danced and lit up the cabin. He shivered and wondered when morning would come with Wild Jack and his Pa to find him and take him home. But the wind spoke louder than his mnd and soon all he could concentrate on was the cold and the wind and he lay back down and tossed and turned in a restless sleep, his thoughts scheming a plan for blankets and food.

Even though it was dark, the snow was luminous. He plowed through, pushed one leg forward then tugged the other. When he sank to his chest, he pulled himself out, grasping at anything that would hold — rocks or branches, tree trunks or crusted snow. He fought his way over small hills and tumbled down ravines until he rolled onto the river ice. It was darker then. Oh, it was darker then — pitch black. Something about the trees and the snow. But on the cold flat barren ice, there was only the wind and the blackness wrapping tightly around him like a blanket that was cold. He pulled his hood more tightly over his head and started out, leaving the swaying and boxing trees behind him.

He felt as if he'd been walking in the darkness forever, one step at a time, one foot after the other, slowly, a struggle, his legs reluctant to move, looking for any sign of the sleigh. He didn't know what time it was or how long he'd been searching — it seemed like his whole life, as if he'd always been alone in the storm. And then he saw it — like a ghost. Snow piled in small drifts, the canvas over the sleigh's bed flapping violently, whipped by the wind, clapping against the side of the sleigh like an apparition laughing at his efforts.

He looked to where the hole in the ice had been. It wasn't a hole anymore, more like a wound that had scarred – horseheads frozen statues jumping from the ice, eyes fixed in shrieking horror and fear, the reigns that Wild Jack had cut trailing from the sleigh into the ice.

He ignored the horses, untied the canvas, threw it back, and rustled through the provisions until he found what he was looking for — two horse blankets and more cheese. Then he turned back out across the ice, moving more swiftly now, the deed being done. Soon the trees hovered in front of him and he searched for his path. He recognized the shape of the shoreline and found a fading trail — an echo from the wind, a small wrinkle in the otherwise smooth waves and drifts of snow, a line of tiny craters trickling into the forest.

He stuffed the cheese into a pocket, wrapped the blankets around himself like a cloak, and climbed the hill. In some places, behind a large rock or in a small valley, the wind had not erased his trail, but mostly it was gone. He put each foot forward expecting solid ground only to find an invisible hole that the snow had secretly concealed. He tumbled then picked himself up. Ice crusted his eyebrows and lashes, making it hard to keep his eyes open. He couldn't see, couldn't walk, didn't know where to find the cabin.

Sometime in the night the wind stopped. And from somewhere in his dreams he awoke and it was as if he'd never slept. He sensed the change — could hear it through the silence in the room. There was no voice from the wind whistling about. It had moved on. And the cabin was filled with brightness. It invaded every corner and crevasse. He got up and looked outside — the sky so blue that it shimmered between the trees and on the snow as if each flake were alive, covering the branches like sleeves and sculpting the ground into a rolling plain.

He decided to head home. Why wait to be rescued? On a clear day, it wasn't that far. And he'd been on ice all his life — playing and skating and fishing and harvesting to fill the icehouses. He put on his hat, gloves, and coat, then stepped outside. It was early and the sun lingered low in the southeast. The air was cool and crisp and he inhaled it deeply before plowing through the snow. He weaved his way between the trees and lost sight of the cabin. Within the solitude of the forest, all the sounds were muted and distant. Only his labored breathing and the swish of his legs forging through the deep snow penetrated the muffled stillness of the wintry wood.

He climbed to the top of a ridge and looked down through the barren trees to the frozen river below — cold and flat and white, the other islands small snow-covered mounds frozen in place by time and capped with a dome of blue. And there was the sleigh, alone on the ice, a grey stain. And to the left, Clayton shimmered on the horizon between ice and sky — an inversion of red and greens and browns — out of place in a world of blue and white. He stumbled down the hill.

When he reached the ice, it was even brighter — the snow sparkled pure and brilliant. He squinted his eyes to the point where his muscles hurt and spots danced across his view. He walked out onto the ice far enough to get beyond the deep drifts along the shore and then turned downriver toward home — the ice booming around him, expanding in the sun, and he knew it was a good sign.

In the distance he spotted two horses approaching — tall thin sticks rising between Hemlock and Grenell. As they came nearer, he recognized his father and Wild Jack. He started running and jumping and waving his arms.

"Pa! Jack!"

The horses galloped up, snow billowing around their forelegs, their studded shoes crunching into the ice.

His father jumped off his horse and embraced him. "Are you all right?"

"Yes, I'm fine."

"He's a man before his time," Jack said.

His father hugged him again before lifting him onto the horse and climbing on himself. His father held him with one arm, shook the reins with the other, and swung the horse. They trotted downriver, the only things moving on the ice. He imagined what they looked like from afar — black specks against a sea of white. But he didn't feel alone. He was with his father and Wild Jack and he was on his way home.

II

And then it was spring. White frosting melted from rooftops and the deep mounds of snow that blanketed the fields shrank until they were only thin white sheets. Small knolls appeared, green islands in a sea of white until the last snow was thrown back as from a bed in the freshness of a spring morning and daffodils and crocuses popped open in fields of dappled sunlight.

And the frozen river, once a solid tundra of flat expanse, softened into gray puddles as the insides of each crystal melted away leaving only fragile and delicate skeletons of honeycomb ice. Wind tossed waters heaved and cracked the weakening ice sheets along already jagged shores, pushing fields and flows into open bays where they rolled and crashed and resonated over the islands.

The air came alive with sounds. Ben first noticed it as he lay in his bed by the open window — peepers and bullfrogs croaking, crows cawing, and robins twittering. Spring rains roared on the rooftop and dropped in torrential waterfalls off the eaves. And after the thunder rumbled and rolled away in the quick winds of a spring squall, the root filled earth slurped and gargled and squeaked as it drank like a growing boy thirsty after a long hard day of work.

He and his father tilled the fields, turning new soil in preparation for seed. He led the horses — two young mares that his father had bought to replace the two that fell through the ice — and his father manned the plow. And then one evening they went fishing.

His father was on the front porch in his rocking chair filling a lantern with kerosene as Ben came up the steps from the barn where he'd been milking the cows.

"Go fetch the bamboo poles and a bucket, Ben. Your Ma wants us to catch some bullheads."

He walked around the side of the house to the cellar door. He lifted it up and over then descended into the shadowy room. The bamboo poles hung on the far wall. He jumped and hopped across the puddled dirt floor. Old dry cobwebs stretched, broke, and fell into his hair and onto his arms as he lifted the poles off the wall. He swiped the strands away as he weaved his way back to the light at the stairs, grabbing a bucket on his way out.

His father was waiting on the porch with the lantern and a can of night crawlers. Together they marched down the path to the river in the fading light of day, the bamboo poles bouncing on his shoulder, the bucket swinging in his hand. It was nearly dark by the time they reached their spot just above the marsh.

They sat on an old log they'd dragged there years before — though it seemed to Ben that it had been there forever. A light breeze blew gently and small ripples lapped the shore. He could smell the swamp — seaweed and dead fish. It always filled the marsh — sweet yet damp. His father lifted the globe of the lantern, flicked a match, and lit the wick. Then he set it down in front of them, close to the water in the short spring grass, its glow shimmering on the bay.

Ben unwound the line from his pole and had his bob and baited hook in the water before his father. Almost immediately his line tugged and the bob dipped beneath the surface. He whipped his pole back and lifted a bullhead out. He seized the line just above the fish's mouth and wrapped his fingers around the head, careful not to get stung by the horns as he removed the hook. He'd been careless before and felt the sharp pain of a bullhead's prods. His hand had swollen to twice its normal size and had been useless for over a week. He tossed the fish into the bucket

Between Ben and his father, they soon had a full catch. They wrapped the lines around the poles. His father lifted the bucket of bullheads and Ben picked up the lantern. The light flooded the water and the edge of cattails and swamp grass that made up the marsh. Something floating in the water caught Ben's eye and he walked down the shoreline to investigate.

"What do you see?"

"There's something strange floating in the water."

His father followed him to the water's edge.

"See it, Pa? It looks like there's snakes crawling around it."

"Let me see that lantern." His father lifted the lantern high above his head.

"It almost looks like a horse, Pa. But it's green and too big."

"It is a horse, Ben. It's one of those two spotted mares that fell through the ice. And those snakes are eels nesting inside it."

He strained his eyes to see beyond the edge of darkness and saw his father was right. He'd once fed and taken care of that horse — loved it. Now it was bloated and swollen to almost twice its normal size. And the once warm and smooth coat that he'd curried since a boy was shining green from algae in the lantern's light — rotted through in some places. Eels slid and slithered in and out and over and around each other. He could almost hear them slide.

"I've seen enough Pa. Can we go home?"

He didn't sleep well that night — his mind racing with the horses he had known, that he'd seen drown in the icy waters, and now seen in death's decay. He thought about the eels, eating the insides out and surviving off the horses' demise. And when he fell asleep, he didn't know it, for his thoughts became the dreams of his restless sleep.

In the morning his father went to Clayton. There would be no work in the fields. After he milked and fed the animals, he walked to Eel Bay. His thoughts had become absorbed with the horse and the eels and he wanted to see it in the light of day. But when he reached the fishing log, the horse and the eels were gone. A light wind blew out of the bay from the east bringing the smell of the swamp and he realized the carcass had drifted out of the bay. There was no sign of its having been there, as if it had never been there, but he knew that it had, even though there was no trace.

In the light, he saw the marsh was filled with life. The cattails were a fresh green and a female mallard swam by the reeds. As he explored the water's edge searching for the carcass, he saw two water snakes and several frogs. He thought of the peepers that sang at night — so many of them that not one could be distinguished above the others.

When his father returned that evening, Ben sensed something was wrong. His father's hat was low and his eyes cast down in the shadow of his brim. Even the horse walked with a trodden and tired cadence. His mother came out onto the porch to greet him. His father removed his hat. "I've got some bad news." He fidgeted with the brim of the hat. "Wild Jack was hit by a steamer while rowing his skiff back from Clayton last night. We just spent the whole day looking for him, but never found him."

"Then maybe he's still alive," his mother said.

"No, I don't think so. We scoured the river and checked every island. Sam Broward and some others are still searching the shorelines, but there's no sign of him. Only the shattered remains of his skiff. The river's taken him."

"How could he not see a steamer?" his mother asked.

"Drunk, no doubt."

For a week, he and his father worked shorter hours in the field. The rest of the days were spent searching. They motored up to Round Island in the runabout and over to Grenell and Hemlock and Maple and circled all the islands in between. They walked along the shores, over rocky rubble, and waded in the cold spring water to get around thick brush or bushy willow trees that spread their branches out over the river. When they came to a marsh, they skirted around and then came back later with the runabout to search through the cattails and reeds.

"Remember that spotted mare?" his father said.

"Yeah."

"Just be prepared. That's what Wild Jack might look like if we find him. And the more time that goes by, the worse it will be. But don't be frightened, Ben. It's just the way of things."

But they didn't find Wild Jack and the fields needed to be tilled. Each day seemed brighter than the day before — each afternoon hotter. Ben took off his shirt as he worked with his father in the fields and as the days passed his skin tanned under his sweating brow.

"Gee," he said to the horses. "Haw."

III

And then it was May. The trees were flush with blossoms and buds bursting forth with their fresh green leaves. It was midmorning and he and his father were in the barn when they heard the dinner bell ring in the distance.

"Something must be wrong," his father said. "It can't be but ten o'clock."

When they reached the house, Sam Broward was standing next to his Model A chatting with Ben's mother. "They've found Jack's body," he said. "We were hoping we could borrow your runabout to go fetch it."

"I'll go," his father replied.

"No need for that."

His father's jaw stiffened and it seemed to Ben that even his lips struggled to move. "He's family."

"He's up in a boathouse in Spicer's."

"Can I help?" Ben asked.

"I think not," his mother said.

His father glanced up and away before his gaze fell to his mother. "It's one of those things he needs to know." And his mother's head sank. "It's won't be pleasant, Ben. Do you think you can handle it?"

Ben nodded his head. "I think so."

"Good."

Ben climbed into the car with his father and Sam and they started down the dirt road, dust rolling behind them, Ben bouncing on the back seat.

"Word is spreading pretty quickly," Sam shouted above the roar of the car. "George has gone down to the cemetery to dig the grave."

"Ben and I will go fetch the body," his father said. "You go find a tarp or something to wrap it in. Where'd you say it was?"

"Up in Spicer's Bay in the only brown boathouse there."

The road swung around a small hill and the river appeared below the high bank. The tires skidded in the gravel as Sam stopped the car. Ben and his father climbed out.

"We'll meet you here," his father said. "You'd better find a truck or a wagon too."

They walked down the wooden stairs that led to the boathouse. The door was cockeyed in the jamb and his father forced it open. Inside it was dark and dusty. The runabout bobbed in its slip. Swallows glided in and out, trying to reach their nests, but were too scared by Ben and his father.

Ben untied the lines while is father primed the engine by putting gas in the petcock and cranking the flywheel. The engine churned, spitting at first then slowing to a smooth murmur harmonizing with the bubbling exhaust as his father closed the petcock. With a quick jerk, the boat started out of the slip.

His father steered upriver. It was a calm day, the sky clear and blue. As his father opened the motor up, the bow lifted and planed off, riding over the water, the river splashing away and rolling into the wake behind them.

Fifteen minutes later they entered Spicer's Bay. His father slowed and the wake surged and rolled under the boat. They approached the outside dock of the only brown boathouse in the bay. Long before they neared the dock, though, he noticed the smell. At first it seemed like seaweed and dead fish, but as they docked the boat, and he jumped from the bow with the line, it became stronger and too sour for fish. His father stopped the engine and Ben tied the lines.

"What's that smell, Pa?"

"I'm afraid it's Wild Jack. Remember what I told you, Ben. This is not a pleasant job."

He thought of the horse in Eel Bay, but this smell was worse.

Perhaps it was the dead calm air.

"Let's go up to the house and tell the owner we're here."

He followed his father and stood behind him at the door. "We're here to get Jack Coffin's body," his father said.

"It's tied up in the boathouse. The door is unlocked," the man said.

"Thanks." They turned and started back to the dock.

"Oh, and be sure to leave the rope he's tied with. It's one of the few I own."

"No problem," his father mumbled. "I've got an extra line in my boat."

As they approached the dock house again, they were enveloped by the stale stank air. It filled his lungs with a depressing congestion that affected his very soul.

"Let's back the boat into the boathouse," his father said.

They untied the boat, climbed in, and together maneuvered it around the corners of the dock. Ragged and torn canvas strips hung over the opening to the boathouse in an attempt to keep the swallows out. He pushed the flaps aside as they slid the runabout, stern first, into the slip. Immediately the air was thicker and heavier and he could hardly breathe.

Floating face down in the back of the slip was Wild Jack's bloated body. He felt nauseated. It didn't look like Wild Jack; it didn't even look like a body. The torso was as big as a barrel, the arms and legs as wide as nail kegs, the skin covered with algae — wet, shiny, slick like on a shoreline rock. They guided the boat closer.

"We'll do this as quickly as possible, but it'll be unpleasant." His father reached under the bow for a rope. Then he went to the stern and leaned out over the water. He seized the line tied to Wild Jack and pulled his body toward the boat. He grabbed one arm firmly — as if it were only a stick floating in the water. Ben knew that he would have avoided touching it altogether, but his father

57

untied the rope that held Wild Jack confidently, with all his fingers, and Ben knew he would have tried to untie it with only two or three.

His father tied their rope around Wild Jack. Ben took the old rope from his father and quickly flung it onto the dock. His father finished tying the body then started the engine. The boat shimmied forward and they inched out of the slip, Jack's body pulled behind them, the smell of rotting flesh lingering even with the light breeze. They slowly cruised out of Spicer's Bay, but the stink could not be escaped.

Sam and a small crowd of men met them at the boathouse. The air quickly soured. His father untied the rope from the boat that held Jack's body and handed it off. The body was floated around the outside dock until it bounced on the shore. Some of the men took their shoes and socks off, so Ben took his off too and rolled up his pant legs. Others unfolded the tarp. Ben waded into the water. It was cold and icy and numbed his feet. He grabbed the line and started untying it from Jack.

"Ben!" his father shouted. "You don't have to do that."

"It's okay, Pa. I don't mind." It was Wild Jack after all.

He had the rope off and he held Wild Jack's body from drifting away. The skin was cold and slimy. His father led the others into the water. They slid the canvas under Jack's body and rolled it around him. Ben handed them the line he had removed and they used it to tie the canvas tight around the body. Ben thought the stench would be tied in too, but it seeped out through the wet canvas cloth.

Everyone squeezed around the rolled canvas and lifted it out of the water. They laid it on the shoreline while they put their shoes back on, streams of water rolling out toward the river. They struggled up the narrow stairs, four men on each side. Ben balanced himself between the edge of the stairs and the wet tarp. With each step he felt as if he was going to fall but he made it to the top without faltering. Water dripped from the tarp and dotted their path. They laid the body on the back of a truck. Ben, his father, and Sam got into the Model A. The fresh clean air swept through the open windows as they bounced down the dirt road. Ben inhaled it deeply.

When they reached the cemetery, George Lanning and two other men were finishing the grave. Wild Jack's body was carried over. Ben stood next to his father as the body was lowered. Once again his nostrils burned from the smell. He had thought that he might get used to it, like the smell of a dog that's been sprayed by a skunk. But he knew he would never get used to death.

He went to one of the shovels standing stiffly in the mound of dirt. He tossed the first bit of soil onto the canvas-covered body. His father and George followed — each shovel crunching into the loose ground before the dirt was returned to the earth.

The gray canvas tarp disappeared and then there was only Ben, his father, and the men. The smell of Wild Jack's body — the stench of death itself — faded away in the breeze. And he felt he'd been alive forever and always would be — like the river and the wind.

Dust and Water

She searched through the window to the river below, hoping for an approaching beacon, red or green, on the water, but all she could see were the trees in front brightened by the glow from inside. Hers was the only light — all the other cottages and islands were empty and dark. She stared at herself in the plate glass for several minutes, her focus falling somewhere in the blackness over the river as she imagined what the house looked like from the water. Soft and inviting, isolated and alone.

Thanksgiving was next week. She wanted to do something

special before she abandoned the river for the winter, so she planned a dinner party, made paper for invitations and penciled them with different river scenes for each of her guests. The invitations said six o'clock, but now she wished she'd put five or even four — anytime before the darkness set in. Dusk dropped so suddenly, making each evening an eternity. She couldn't believe it had been four months since her brother's death. It was still as near to her as the boat's hull slapping at the rough water down at the dock. But soon her friends would be here.

She'd cooked a feast, more food than they could possible eat — turkey, mashed potatoes, wild rice dressing, corn, peas, squash, and homemade cranberry sauce. But she'd really indulged with the desserts. It had taken three days to bake it all — chocolate banana bread, pumpkin squares, and several pies. It kept her busy, kept her mind off things. She scattered hors d'oeuvres around the house like potpourri until a bowl sat on every table — chips and French onion dip; celery, broccoli florets, and curry dip; nuts and popcorn and Chex mix. She extended the leaves on the old oak table and arranged the candlesticks, cloth napkins, and place settings on the nice linen.

She heard a boat slow — washing out of nowhere. She hurried to the window and saw the red and green lights nose into the dock. She recognized the low rumble, the spread of bow lights, the height of the stern light. It was Eric and Claire in his parents' Hutchinson. She dried her hands on her pants, slipped on her shoes, and scooted down the path.

"Hello, hello," her voice squeaked — as if she were an old woman cooped up, alone, desperate for company. It surprised her. Even though she felt older, as if she were wiser than her days, she knew better.

"We came a little early in case you needed help," Claire said. She clasped the ribband on the dock, high from low water, and clambered out, her short blonde hair bouncing.

"And we brought an apple pie." Eric handed it up to Mia before climbing out himself, his dark hair sweeping across his forehead, blending with the night.

"Oh, you didn't have to, but thank you." She clasped the covered plate. "You arrived just in time. There's nothing else to do and I just finished peeling the potatoes. C'mon up and have a drink." She tied their bowline and led them up the path.

She set the apple pie on the dessert table with her pumpkin and pecan pies. Eric wandered from room to room testing each bowl's offerings as he waited for his beer. "This is a real tasty spread, Mia."

"No kidding," Claire added. "You've outdone yourself on this one. The table's set; the food is cooking; there's absolutely nothing I can do?"

"Exactly as I planned it." Mia laughed uneasily, betraying her anxiety, but both Eric and Claire seemed not to notice. "Relax, enjoy." She handed them their drinks, then heard a boat and recognized the high-pitched whine of a Mercury. "It sounds like Mark's here." She moved toward the door. "Make yourselves at home. I'll go greet him!" She ran down to the dock.

"I'm so relieved you're here," she said as she bound onto the dock.

"Yeah? Why's that?" He tossed his lines and jumped up in one movement.

"I don't know. This might be more than I can handle."

She tied his stern line while he tied the bow, then she stepped up to him and folded her arms around his chest and nuzzled her cheek into his fleece, wishing he'd reciprocate. He did, wrapped his arms around her, but it was light and distant and brotherly, polite without any of the passion she longed for. Cursory. And when he let go, she knew she had to as well.

They strolled up the path.

"Did your brother get here?" Mark asked.

"Yeah, earlier this afternoon. And he promptly went out on the river. Haven't seen him since."

As they stepped inside, Eric lifted a picture frame off the mantle. "What year was this picture taken? Was it last year?"

"Yeah." Mia's eyes skimmed the image in the photo. "At the Halloween party." She wore an old round aluminum sled on her head painted like a mushroom cap.

Andy appeared in the door with a knock, a bottle of wine in his hand, and his mop of long, loosely-curled hair bobbing on his head. It surprised Mia because she hadn't heard his boat, but she was relieved too, relieved that she was distracted enough not to notice.

"What a gorgeous night!" he said. "Your place is the only light on the river."

Eric placed the picture back on the mantle. "Hey, what took you so long?"

"Putting the bike up."

"That ol' Harley still working? I never saw you on it this year."

"Oh, yeah, but keeping it in tune is half the fun of it."

"Sounds like guy talk to me. I need to check the turkey." Mia moved toward the kitchen.

"I'll help you."

As she and Claire went into the kitchen, the guys continued their talk about motorcycles. Mia opened the stove and wondered why they did such reckless things. If only her brother hadn't driven full crank down the channel that night. If only he'd been wearing a life jacket.

Claire's hand touched her shoulder. "Are you all right?" Claire asked.

"Yeah." She reached in with the mitts and removed the turkey. "I was only thinking."

"What can I do?"

"Why don't you drain those potatoes and mash 'em while I make the gravy?" The turkey pan clanked on the stove. "I'll put this turkey on a cutting board and get one of the guys to trim it."

"What about Miles?" Claire asked. "Is he coming?"

"He's supposed to, but he's off doing his own thing. I wouldn't be surprised if he blew me off."

She transferred the turkey and carried it out to the table.

Andy paused at the sight of the turkey but, animated by his story, kept on talking, "…into the turn doin' fifty-five and the whole bike swung right around until the rear wheel was practically in front of me. But I rode it the whole way. Took a big piece out of my jeans and leather jacket, but that was the key — just stayin' on it."

"Yeah, well that's the true mark of a Harley rider," Eric said. "Just lean the other way and it'll right itself."

"Can someone cut the turkey?" Mia sheepishly interrupted.

Mark straightened up from where he was leaning against the mantle. "I will."

"Thanks." She returned to the kitchen. "Good grief," she said with a sigh. "They're sharing near-death experiences."

"Try not to let it bother you," Claire said. "Boys'll be boys. Do you have an electric mixer?"

"In that cupboard." She pointed then spooned the grease out of the roasting pan, scooped in some sour cream and flour, and whisked to the whine of the mixer, taking her time in the hope that Miles might show. But she was finally faced with the inevitable and she brought the entrées to the table.

"Dinner is served," she announced. She lit the candles and dimmed the lights while her guests found their seats. She slipped into the spot next to Mark, standing behind her chair, inspecting the table. It was then she noticed the two extra place settings — one for Miles, but she'd miscounted. "Oops," she said, glancing from end to end. "Too many plates."

"Well, maybe Miles will still show up," Claire said. "And the other spot can be for any wayfaring sailors that might put in."

Just then they heard the hum of a boat washing into the dock.

"Speak of the devil," Claire added.

"It'll give us time to pour the wine. Here." Mia grabbed the large bottle of Chardonnay from the center of the table and handed it to Mark. "Pour this."

Two minutes later, Miles opened the door, a bottle of Moosehead in his hand.

"Nice of you to join us, Miles," Mia said.

"I hope you didn't wait."

"We just sat down."

Miles surveyed the table, his mouth drooped in a frown. Mia couldn't recall a single time he'd laughed in four months.

"What did you do, Mia? Forget Blair was dead?"

Claire came to her defense. "She was busy preparing this meal while you were out communing with the river."

"Sit down, Miles," Mark said. "So we can eat."

"Yes." Mia handed the plate of turkey to Mark. "Start passing things around. Fill yourselves up. There's tons of food."

Miles sat at the other end of the table closest to the door.

"How much longer are your parents keeping the cottage open?" Eric asked, gestured toward the ceiling. "This place must be hard to heat."

Mia glanced up and the knots in the pine boards were like stars to wish upon.

"Mom and Dad are coming up next week," Miles said as if it were a command. Mia knew it was directed at her.

Claire spooned some squash onto her plate. "Oh, well, it won't be long and it'll be spring again."

"Doesn't seem like it was that long ago," Andy remarked. "And still, it's further behind us than it is in front. Isn't that something?"

"That's the truth. It flies by when you're not thinking about it." Claire passed the squash to Eric.

"Yup." Miles clanked his fork. "And before you know, we'll all be dead."

The statement shook Mia. "Miles! Do you have to be so gloomy?"

"Hey, I'm just trying to keep a perspective on things."

"Well maybe it's the wrong perspective," Mia countered.

"You know, he predicted his death," Eric said.

"And just how did he do that?" Miles scoffed.

Eric finished chewing his food. "We were siding a house and we decided to sign the back of one of the boards. And I said, 'We'll all be old timers by the time someone sees this.' And he said, 'Not me. I won't make it past thirty.'"

"Ah," Miles jeered. "He had a death wish. Of course you can predict it if you're serious enough about it."

"He was just reckless," Mark said.

"Whatever. We all saw it coming."

"Not me," Mark responded. "And there isn't a day that goes by when I don't think if only I had done something different that day."

Miles picked up his beer and pointed the mouth of the bottle at Mark. "Well, you should get over that."

"Like you?" Mia said.

"What the hell is that supposed to mean?"

"Oh, come on Miles. You know exactly what I'm talking about. Let's be honest and put it out there."

"Put what out there?" Claire asked.

"Blair saved Miles's life that night," Mia blurted. "Grabbed him by the arm and shoved him overboard."

"How do you know I wasn't thrown by the boat turning at the last moment?"

"What? Are you changing your story now that you've had

67

some time to digest it?"

"He didn't save my life. He almost killed me. I told him to slow down."

Mia took a deep breath and glanced around the room — this was not what she had planned and no one was eating. She reached for her glass of wine, the foot chiming against her plate as she raised it, the first and only sound. But then Mark came to her rescue.

"I think we need a toast."

"Yes, yes," Claire piped. "A toast." She reached for her glass.

Mark raised his. "To Mia's fine meal and the coming together of friends along the river." The clinking of glasses rang out above the table. "Was it an old house?" Mark asked. "The one you were siding? Were there a lot of cut nails?"

"Yeah. Why?" Eric said.

"There was a square nail in his ashes."

"And how would you know that?" Miles snapped.

"I showed him," Mia said.

"You did? What would Mom and Dad say?"

"What's it matter? No one was doing anything about them. They were just sitting up under the bow of the boat all summer. I thought they might get wet and soggy so I took them out. Mark was here, so we looked through them."

"You still have his ashes?" Eric asked. "What are you going to do with them?"

"Mom and Dad talk about throwing them in the river," Mia said. "Maybe next week when they're here to close the cottage."

"I think Blair would have liked being in the bow of a boat." Claire nodded her head. "That's where he tried to spend his life."

"What do they look like?" Andy asked. "I've never seen anyone's ashes before."

"They're hard to describe. Would you like to see them?" She

68

was enthusiastic — eager to show them.

"You can't show them his ashes," Miles barked.

"Why not? We're all friends." She felt emboldened by his protest and went over to the buffet, opened the doors, and found the box. It was small, but heavy for its size, about as big as a shoebox, made of thick, plain, brown cardboard.

"That's it?" Andy said. "Did they come like that?"

"Yeah." She passed it to Claire. "They told us we could do whatever we wanted with them when we picked them up."

"They're heavier than I imagined." Claire lifted and lowered the box with her palm. "And smaller."

"Can I look inside?" Andy took the box from Claire.

"Sure. It's already open."

"I object."

"Why?" Mia said. "You're going to see them when we spread them on the river.

Andy gently lifted the cardboard flaps and pulled out the plastic bag. He pushed his plate aside and laid the bag on the table. It was mostly bone fragments — white and shades of grey, the finer dust settled at the bottom.

"Feel them if you want," she said. "We looked through them for teeth but didn't find any — just that old nail."

Andy opened the bag slowly.

"What are you doing?" Miles questioned.

"Looking through them," Andy said. He pinched a small amount and dropped it back. Then he sifted through it like it was a cereal box with a prize. Within a minute he stopped. It was silent. His fingers were covered with dust. He snickered, "Should we have communion?" He reached into the bag and raised an offering of ashes. "The body of Blair."

"That's it. That's enough." Miles jumped from his seat and lunged around the table. He snatched the bag and darted out the door.

"Miles!" Mia yelled. She chased after him, stumbling down the path with only the glow of the house to guide her. When she reached the dock, Miles was out on the end, dumping the ashes into the river, shaking the bag like a rug. "Miles," she murmured.

"There. That's done."

"What *will* Mom and Dad say?"

The others approached the landing, keeping their distance. Mia navigated across the dock and stood next to Miles. She peered into the river. Most of the ashes were sinking, disappearing into the murky depths, but some floated on the surface like stardust on the water, drifting away into the darkness.

The Midnight Lady

I remember the first time Pa told how to rob the Clayton bank. It was years ago — the year they took the farm. Earl and I were just kids.

We were at the Pastime on a Sunday afternoon in the back playing checkers listening to a Yankee game on Harry's radio. Harry was behind the bar with a rag in his hand. He always had a rag in his hand, ready to wipe down the bar. He kept filling Pa's glass with whiskey, saying, "I sure am sorry about your farm, Mitch."

And Pa kept throwin' the whiskey down his throat. "Don't you worry about ol' Mitch," he slurred. He was sittin' on one of the high stools, left elbow on the bar. He reached for his drink with his other hand. "Ol' Mitch has a plan. I'll get those bastards." And he took another slug.

"That's good to hear, Mitch. No sense lettin' 'em get you down." Harry wiped the bar. "Not many people could rebound so quickly after that kind of blow."

Joe Spalding was playing pool with Silent Ernie. He lined up a shot and said, "What are you going to do? What's your plan?" The balls clicked.

Silent Ernie watched while leaning on his pool stick opposite Joe waiting for his chance to shoot.

"I'm goin' to rob that bank," Pa said proudly.

Joe laughed out loud as he lined up his next shot. Harry cracked a smile as he continued to wipe the bar. Silent Ernie just stared at the balls rolling around the table.

"How you goin' do that, Mitch?" Harry asked.

Pa turned slowly on his stool to look at Harry, left elbow still on the bar. "I'll tell ya how I'm going to do it, Harry," he slurred. "I'm goin' to do it by boat in a fog. As soon as there's a good thick fog, I figure I'll go up there and rob the place. It's fool proof. How would they catch you in a boat in a fog?"

"Sure, Mitch. And you'll just go back to Wellesley and spend out the rest of your days."

The crowds were cheering in Yankee stadium, but I'd lost track of the game.

"You guys think I'm nuts. I know you do. But that's only because you guys don't have any guts."

But neither did Pa. He never robbed the bank and he ended up working as a mason for Joe. But I never forgot about his plan.

* * * * * * * * *

"How much further do you think it is?" I ask.

"It should be right in front of us," Earl says.

"I think I see Calumet." I squint into the fog.

"Where?"

"Right there." I point across the port bow.

"It can't be over there."

"No sense arguing 'bout it, boys," Pa would say if he were here. He'd be standing between Earl and me, laughing, while letting us navigate through the fog.

We scour the shadows trying to discern the tower on Calumet. The fog is thick and gray. Even the four bags of cash in the stern are hard to see. Earl turns the boat slightly upriver, guiding it with a compass toward Grindstone where our boat is hidden.

We finally find Grindstone Island, I think near Aunt Jane's Bay, and follow its shoreline downstream. Through the haze it's like a black and white photograph — a silhouette off the port side. Earl guides *The Midnight Lady* through the Picton Channel, around Point Angiers and into Plumtree Marsh. We're both silent. I think he sees Pa between us too. I can hear Pa telling us what to do, still drunk from the night before.

"Nose her in slowly. Get up on the bow, Dell."

Earl and I were bullhead fishing one evening in the bay when I reminded him of Pa's idea.

"Pa had a great many ideas and schemes," he said.

"Well, this was one of his best. We've never done business with the Clayton bank, not since the foreclosure. And we were both a lot younger then. So they wouldn't know who we were by our voices and of course we'd wear masks."

He didn't say anything, just kept staring at the river, rocking on his seat.

"So what do you think, Earl?"

He smacked his lips while considering it. "It's too early in the spring. They'd recognize the boat."

We were one of the few people with a boat in the water already — just a little jon boat for fishin' and trappin'.

"I didn't mean this week, Earl." We'd wait until the ice was completely out. And we'd need to plan ahead."

"They still might recognize the boat, Delbert."

I pondered that for a moment. The river flowed by. Some flow ice further in the bay roared in the breeze. The peepers trilled. Soon the trees would blossom.

"What if we had another boat — one they wouldn't recognize?"

"How are we going to do that?"

I looked at him with a big grin. "We'll steal one." And then I started to laugh.

* * * * * * * * * *

The Midnight Lady was long, slick, and fast. She was a running boat in the twenties, her hull black as pitch, almost magically invisible at night, an illusion slicing through the water. But she'd spent some time at the bottom with seventy gallons of moonshine in her bow. Russ Martin was bringing her back from Gan in the fall when he hit Jackstraw. It was one of those November nights when the river plays tricks on people — even on Russ, who'd known the river all his life.

I didn't tell Earl we were taking *The Lady* 'til that morning. He'd done all the work on her when Old Man Henry pulled her out of the river. It was a mess. But Earl loved the work. He made *The Midnight Lady* like new.

"This is it. This is it," I whispered loudly as I shook him in his bed. A cold spell had moved in the day before and it had started to rain in the night. Everything had turned to mist and then to thick fog — the river, the trees, even the earth itself. We'd been waiting for it all spring.

"What's the hurry, Dell? The bank doesn't open 'til nine."

"Do you plan on stealing a boat at ten, Earl?"

"What boat do you plan on stealing anyways, Delbert? It won't be that hard."

"We're going to take *The Lady*."

"What!? We can't take our neighbor's boat."

"That's the whole point, Earl. Since you restored it, no one will suspect us."

"What are you talking about, Dell. That's exactly why they'll suspect us."

* * * * * * * * * *

Our runabout is pulled up on shore and tied to a big willow tree close to the marsh. Earl slows down.

"Meet me over at the quarry," I say as he noses *The Lady* toward shore.

"The Picton Quarry? Why there?"

"We're going to fill this boat with stones and sink her."

"Sink her?" he yells. "We are not! We're not sinking *The Lady*!"

"Simmer down, Earl. We've got to destroy all the evidence, every trace."

"*The Lady* isn't evidence. It's a boat. We'll just tie her up and let 'em find her."

"We've got to sink her, Earl. Don't you see? What's it matter now anyways? We're set."

"She's too beautiful a boat to sink, Dell. Now you get that notion out of your head."

"You're not gettin' sentimental on me now, are you Earl? Let's keep our heads straight. If you can't do it, I will. You get the runabout." I nudge him gently away from the wheel, but he shoves me back and pushes the throttle down.

"We're not sinking this boat."

He banks the boat out of the bay. I lose my balance for a second.

"What the hell are you doing, Earl? Have you lost your mind? We're in a fog!" I lose sight of land and have no idea where we are. We're completely surrounded by the mist with the throttle of *The Midnight Lady* wide open. "Slow down!" I yell.

"Not if we're going to sink this boat!"

I try to take the wheel and slow the throttle, but he thrusts me away.

"Okay. Okay," I say. "We won't sink the boat." But it's too late. I feel the rumble of rock on wood and metal. I'm thrown forward. We're lucky we're not killed. I think it's Shark's Tooth, but nothing looks right in a fog. It feels like we're spinning, but we're not moving at all. Earl has a cut in his forehead. It's a little bloody. The boat is high and dry.

"Now look what you've done, Earl."

"At least she won't sink," he says and he wipes the blood from his forehead with his sleeve.

There's nothing to do but wait for the fog to lift and we don't say anything else. I know we've had it. I watch the droplets drift around us and I can only think of Pa. I know he'd be frustrated with us for arguing, but I think he'd have been proud of us too — just for trying.

When Pipes Freeze

A deep freeze pierced the night. It was sudden — the first one this year. Wisps of mist curl into the morning sun along the shore, hiding from the day, and the water feels harder on the boat.

The wind bites my cheeks and grips my chest around the loose collar of my chamois shirt. I should have worn another layer, it is November after all, but the brightness of the sun and the blueness of the sky fooled me. It's not the first time. Summer is long over and the cottages are yawning, longing to sleep. Soon, the river will freeze up and be covered with a thick layer of ice.

As I pull into the dock, I see Mia's father by the water pump at the river's edge, the cover off the plywood housing, his head somewhere inside. All that shows is the back of his quilted red vest and jeans.

Mia is on the hill pouring steaming water from a kettle onto the exposed pipes on the ground. "Anything yet, Mom?" she yells toward the cottage.

"Not yet, dear."

She shakes the kettle then comes down to the dock. "Our pipes froze last night."

"I see that."

"Do you know anything about frozen pipes?" Mia's father asks. He steps over from the pump, a large crescent wrench in his hand. He is short and stocky with wide shoulders and balding hair.

"Only that they're solid, " I say.

He chuckles. "That part we already know. Mia's brother usually took care of these things." He speaks slowly. I think it strange he doesn't refer to Blair by his name or as his son. "But we're learning. Aren't we, Mia?"

"We need to boil more water." She kneels and reaches over the dock, dunking the kettle under the surface until it is filled.

"He was good at these things," I say.

"Come on up and have some coffee." Mia's father pats my shoulder and we amble off the dock – him, Mia, then me – up the narrow path to the house. She keeps peeking back, grinning from behind strands of hair, and I keep kicking myself for never having the courage to kiss her. But Blair and I were best friends and she was his little sister.

I can't count the number of times she'd caught me looking at her over the years. She'd smile while I quickly looked away — guilty. But the opportunity never came — at least not until this past summer.

I was rafting out in Eel Bay with five or six other boats — just drifting as the sun went down. As it turned out, my little kicker was tied up alongside the boat Mia was in and she climbed over.

"Do you mind if I sit in your boat?" she said. "There's more room to stretch my legs."

I tossed her an old boat cushion and she leaned against the aluminum gunnel and laid one leg across the boat on the hard seat.

A while later, the Coast Guard appeared in the distance and we scattered like scallywags for no good reason. We were all legal with the correct safety and emergency equipment. I'm not sure if they chased anyone or not, but Mia was in my boat, giggling as everyone untied from one another.

We took a long night cruise under a sky full of stars. I think it was the first time I'd ever been alone with her. And a little after midnight I dropped her off at her dock. What else was I going to do? I suppose I could have tried kissing her in my little aluminum boat, but it would have been difficult between the seats.

I jumped out with the lines, and she was climbing out before I'd a chance to tie them. And then we were standing there facing each other, and I thought, now's my chance. It was the moment. Neither of us spoke. We just stood there looking each other in the eye, both of us too shy, too respectful of relationship, long seconds of silence, not awkward, but pensive.

I leaned in, slow motion. She did too. My free hand reached across the gap and touched hers as I veered to the right and pecked her cheek. I didn't have the nerve.

I said good-bye, jumped back into my boat with the lines, and within a week Blair was dead, and everything changed.

* * * * * * * * *

Mia's mother is emptying the refrigerator and organizing items on the counter as we step inside. "Do you need any food, Mark?" she says. "I'm just going to throw it away."

"Thanks, but I'm leaving soon too."

"So your parents are forcing you out as well? That's why we're here — to get Mia out. You young people, sometimes I just don't know. You'd stay here all winter if we didn't come and take you home."

Mia opens a cabinet door and a rush of falling, clanking pots pours out. "We need to boil more than just one kettle of water at a time," she says.

"I think we should just leave it frozen," her mother says. "We need to get a whole new system and frozen, broken pipes would be the perfect excuse."

"Oh, mother."

"I'm serious. And we wouldn't have to waste any more time on it today. It could wait until spring. I love the spring." She looks at me. "I don't need running water to finish cleaning. I'm doing just fine without it."

Mia's father meanders in through the front door. "Now, Margaret," he says. "We can still get a new system in the spring."

"But we won't and you know it, Lyman. Not if we fix this today." She comes over and whispers to me, "I hope we don't get them thawed out." And then she laughs delightfully.

"Have you tried to find where it might be frozen?" I ask.

"I have no idea," Mia says. "I just keep throwing hot water on the pipes."

I try to remember where Blair had problems with freezing. "I think Blair mentioned he had trouble by the pressure tank."

"Why don't you show Dad while I fill this other pot?" She gives me a look that I've grown fond of — a squint of the eyes meant only for me, acknowledging my efforts as a kind of chivalry for her alone.

Just this week, I stopped by after a day of building docks — a summer job that had extended into fall — just to see if she was there, knowing she would be.

80

She was preparing a dinner — as if she knew I'd be by on that last day before her parents arrived to take her away. We ate by candlelight, the only light on the river — that and the shimmer in her eyes.

But our conversation was polite — *"This tastes great."* *"Thanks."* *"How's the dock building going?"* *"It's starting to get cold."* — more silence than words. Once the plates were cleared, I suggested we go for a walk.

We stumbled down the narrow path in the dark. The leaves shuffled. Our hands grazed yet never clasped, touching, pulling back, pinkies teasing.

* * * * * * * * *

Mia heads for the dock as I lead her father outside to the pressure tank near the back door. I have to clear away leaves in order to reach a faucet where the galvanized steel pipe changes to black plastic.

"Don't you pay any attention to Mrs. D.," he says. "She's just a little uneasy. Being here at the cottage brings back too many memories — especially around the holidays. It's hard on her. She just wants to leave soon. I'll get a new system when we need one."

"Who knows, maybe you could use some of these pipes when you get a new system."

He laughs. "I doubt it. It's pretty cob. But it's worked all these years since we bought the cottage — with a little persuasion sometimes, mind you. But you're supposed to rough it at camp."

I turn the handle of the faucet. Water pours out. "Well, it's not frozen between here and the river."

"Geez," he says. "I hope it's not frozen in some wall in the house."

"I doubt it. The house is somewhat heated."

Mia returns from the river. "Did you fix it? I thought I heard water running."

"Not yet, but it's right here." I grab the black plastic pipe. It crunches as I bend it. "This doesn't sound too good. Is the kettle hot enough?"

"I'll go get it," Mia says. She comes running back and pours the steaming water. Creakings and whispers babble from inside, bangings like the house is haunted and demons are hitting the pipes, pops and swishes as the water flows again.

"That's quite a relief," her father says.

"And we didn't need the other pot!" Mia swings the empty kettle at her side sending a sprinkling of water on the dry leaves.

"Best of all," her father says in a low voice, eyeing the cottage, "we don't need a new system. Thanks, Mark." He slaps my shoulder and Mia gives me a quick hug. I savor the moment.

All fall, after the summer people left, the river was ours. But Blair's ghost hexed me. Whenever we were alone, our conversations would turn to him, our mixed memories and disbelief that someone who knew the river so well could hit a buoy — even if it was a slow blinker on a dark night. So it was never just Mia and me alone, but the two of us plus Blair.

On that last night we had alone together, I ached to hold her. We were along the water's edge where the path crossed a small point of exposed rocks. I could hear the water lapping on shore, whispering to me to make a move. I offered my hand to help her down a small ledge, but our fingers parted once she jumped, and then we stood there in the darkness next to the river.

"Are you going to stay much longer?" she asked.

"I don't know. I'll have to find a place to stay either way — that or move back to Lockport with my parents."

"Lockport's not that far from Jamestown. You could find a job there."

"I know." Her town. What more sign did I need?

I gazed at her and she was facing me and the river disappeared into the night. All I had to do was reach across the space between us, caress her cheeks, stroke her hair, pull her close, and I knew she would let me. I could see it in her eyes. But again I choked. I turned and leaped to the next rock, almost gleeful in my clumsiness.

"But what kind of job would allow me to come back here for the summer?" I said, and the river reappeared.

* * * * * * * * *

"We did it, Mom," Mia says.

"I know. I heard." She acts disappointed. "I guess that means I won't be getting a new kitchen. How about lunch, Mark? We have leftover chicken from Thanksgiving. We thought a turkey would be too much trouble for only four people."

"Oh, I don't know. I should probably be going."

"I won't hear of it. You'll eat first."

"It was a big chicken," Mia's father says. He leans on the counter next to his wife, wiping his hands with a paper towel.

"We'll start with dessert," Mrs. D. says. "I'm cleaning the freezer and this rainbow sherbert will melt. Do you like sherbert?"

"Sure."

She spoons the sherbert into four Dixie cups. "Don't mind the paper and plastic. I don't want to dirty any dishes and I didn't think I had any water." She frowns.

"I understand."

"Do you want cranberry sauce, Mark?" Mia's father asks. He's making the sandwiches.

"Please."

He spreads the cranberry sauce on the bread like it's a peanut butter and jelly sandwich and chuckles. "This is how Blair learned to like cranberry sauce. He wouldn't eat it otherwise. Said he didn't like it, so we mixed it with something he did like."

"I've always liked cranberry sauce," I say.

He doesn't seem to hear me. He picks up the plates and takes them to the dining room. Mrs. D. has set the table with all the perishables — pickles, ketchup, mustard, milk, even cereal. We sit.

"It sure has been a beautiful weekend," Mia's father says.

"It's been like this all fall." I glance at Mia as I pick up my sandwich and take a bite.

"We went for a little boat ride yesterday," Mia's mother says dreamily. "Sort of a last spin before we pull the boat. It was nice. The water was so calm and we drove so slowly I could hear each drop of water rush under the boat."

"We watched the sunset over Eel Bay," her father pipes in. "It sure was pretty. And quiet too. I don't think we saw another boat the entire time."

"I've always thought that fall was the best time to be here," I say. "When there's no one else around."

"What are your plans this winter?" Mia's mother asks.

"None, really."

"You sound just like Blair. A young man like yourself should do something with his life."

"Now, Ma," Mia's father says, "Mark is our guest here and he's young yet. Plenty of time."

"I know. I know. It's just... I'm sorry, Mark. Sometimes it seems like such a waste."

Silence fills a pause in conversation. I nibble at my sandwich.

"This is a summer place, for playing," she continues. "You can't make a living here. You kids have got to learn that. I tried to tell..."

"Could you pass the pickles, dear?"

I finish my sandwich.

"Would you like more, Mark?" Mia's father asks.

"No thanks. I really should be going. You have a lot to do."

"Are you sure?" Mia's mother says. "This all has to go. It won't keep over the winter."

"Oh, Mom. You'll never get us to finish that ketchup." Mia glances at me. "I'll walk you to your boat."

"Thanks for lunch." I stand.

"Well, let me get a bag and give you some of this food." Mia's mother starts for the kitchen.

"Oh, no, really. That's all right."

"But I insist." She returns with a large grocery sack already half full. She clears the table by putting all the food into the bag — even the Grape Nuts. "There you go. It'll just get thrown away if you don't take it." She plunks it on the corner of the table near me.

"Thank you." I smile tightly, not knowing what to say.

"Thanks for your help with the pipes." Mia's father shakes my hand. "If it weren't for you, they'd still be frozen."

"I won't thank you for that, Mark. But do have a good winter." Mia's mother gives me a kiss. Then I pick up the bag of food and Mia and I wander down to the dock. I listen to the leaves shuffling at our feet. I purposely walk slowly.

"Look, there's an oak sapling growing out of that pine," she says.

"Where?"

"Up there, high in that tree."

I search where she points. About twenty-five feet up the pine, a small oak branch is coming out of a bird's nest hole.

"That'll never last," I say. "Either that pine will come apart at the seams or the oak will die."

"How do you know? Those two trees might work something out."

"C'mon — how can they work something out?"

"They can't if you're a pessimist."

We're standing on the dock next to my boat. I crouch and

drop the bag of food into the bow. When I stand she kisses me —
our first real kiss, seconds standing still. I study her as she
bounces back.

"I'll miss you," she says.

I look into her eyes. They are striking and bright and blue and
they sparkle wetly. I think she senses I see this because she looks
down. I reach out and push a strand of her long red hair away from
her eyes, enthralled yet frozen with fear – desperate. My hand
slips around her neck and I pull her to me and wrap my arms
around her. She squeezes back, hard, her head against my chest,
and I feel each of her fingers, separate and distinct like ten people
instead of one.

But even that strength isn't enough. The waves slap the dock;
they don't lap. This time of year, nothing has much give — not the
river, not the ground, not the memory of Blair. A breeze wraps
around us and I feel stiff in her embrace, as if everything is
destined to freeze and ice over.

River Murmurs

Spring. The ground wet and spongy with runoff and rain. The air damp and peaty with the compost of fall. The river swollen and surging.

Jake inhaled the thick moist warm air deeply and slowly as he and Bennie and Frank prepared to leave the job site. He tossed his tools into his canvas tote then stared at the river while waiting for Bennie and Frank to finish gathering their tools.

The river had opened up fast and now only the bays were still locked in ice. He was always glad to see the ice go out and the water reappear. He panned the horizon from Fisher's Landing in the east along the coast of T.I. Park on his left past Clayton, Grenell, Hub, and Murray to the Narrows and the mouth of South Bay in the west, the water littered with ice cakes and small floes drifting with the unseen eddies and currents, tinkling and playing in the soft breezes. Small ripples flashed and danced in the gentle movements of a cat's-paw, but a jagged edge of ice still stretched across South Bay from shore to shore, scattered with gray wet spots and holes like Swiss cheese.

"You ready there, Jake?" Bennie's tool bag clattered at his side as he slapped Jake's shoulder.

"Yeah. I was just admiring the approach of spring." He lifted his bag and turned away from the view. Frank joined them at the corner of the cottage and they marched down the middle of the street.

"Will you look at that? Some fool is out there on the ice." Bennie pointed between two cottages toward the foot of the bay.

Their pace slackened. Jake squinted into the distance. He recognized the gait and skip, the hop and jump of the figure.

"That's no person. That's a kid," Frank said.

But Jake realized it was his son before Frank said it — his little son, only seven years old, out on the ice alone, playing. His tool bag clanked on the road and he sprinted toward the shoreline — Frank and Bennie quickly following.

"Harold! Get off that ice!" he bellowed.

Harold, out on the ice, waving and starting toward them — skipping and jumping gleefully.

"Get off the ice!" Jake yelled and flailed his hands, still running, but his son sank and disappeared, was swallowed up by the icy river.

For an instant Jake staggered as if a dagger sliced and gouged into his gut. He lost all sense of his surroundings, was no longer aware of the river or shore, but focused on the spot where his son had just been. He regained his footing and lurched toward the ice.

"No, Jake! Don't do it!" Frank seized his arm and twirled him.

Jake wrenched it back and tore ahead but Bennie grabbed him too. "You can't go out there, Jake."

"I have to," he screamed, fighting against his friends, shaking his arms free only to have them fasten upon him somewhere else. "He'll drown. He can't swim — not in this cold."

"You'll just kill yourself too," Frank yelled. "If the ice couldn't hold *him*, it certainly won't hold you."

"I can't just leave him out there," he wailed.

"Merle's ice punt," Bennie said. "It should be up next to Crawford's boathouse."

They retraced their path along the shore, away from Harold, across wet soft grass and piles of melting snow, Jake not watching where his feet pounded the earth but at the river and the ice and the hole he couldn't see where he knew his son was.

The ice punt was along the shore between two boathouses, bow end on the crusty ice and the stern on the wet draggled ground. They instinctively moved into place, slipping and groping for the gunnels, pushing as soon as their hands were clenched, Jake on one side, Bennie on the other, and Frank in the stern.

They heaved and the punt snapped from its berth in the ice and shore. They pointed it toward Harold's last location, moving as one, runners rattling, the punt almost speeding ahead of them, gaining momentum — hard to keep up with.

"Watch out!" Bennie yelled. "We're coming up on a small hole."

"See it," Frank shouted back.

But Jake was too focused on Harold to respond. His eyes strained to glimpse some movement, the wave of a little hand, a flash of clothing. They glided over the hole, jumping the two feet to the solid ice on the other side.

"Here's another one!" Bennie hollered. "The whole bay's littered with 'em!"

As they approached it, the ice sagged beneath them, slowly at first, hinging beneath Jake's feet, sinking like quick sand. Suddenly the water rushed in and there was nothing but chunks of ice bobbing beneath his feet in the open water. His hands and arms automatically bore his weight and he swung his legs into the boat.

"Grab the oars!" he barked.

"It looks like good ice over there." Frank pointed to the left as he stooped for an oar.

Jake chopped at the water with an oar, splashing and knocking the floe of ice in swirls behind his strokes.

Bennie stepped over the seats to the bow. "Just a little further."

Jake paddled, struggling to propel the punt toward the thicker ice, shouting to Harold all the way. "We're coming Harold! Just hold on!"

At last Bennie hurled himself over the square bow and tugged the punt onto the ice. Jake tossed his oar down and leaped forward. They hauled the punt the rest of the way out of the hole and pivoted it toward the foot of the bay, gaining momentum again, vaulting wet spots and holes for another fifty yards. Jake could clearly see the hole where Harold had fallen, but then they crashed through again and spilled into the punt, Jake's face on the floor. He fumbled up, grappled with an oar, and hacked at the water.

"Maybe over there." Bennie pointed across the open water. Frank paddled on the other side of the punt. They drifted toward the ice. Bennie gingerly tested the ice, yanked on the punt, but the ice gave way beneath his feet and he rolled back in. "It's no good. The ice is bad all around us."

"Then start breaking it," Jake cried. He stumbled to the bow and struck the ice with his oar, straddled the bow, balanced on the gunnel with one foot kicking at the chunks. "Grab the pike pole, grab an oar," Jake ordered. He willed the punt ahead, the cold water seeping into his boot and numbing his toes.

Bennie took the long pike pole and thrust it into the water, deep into the mucky bottom. They crunched into the field, inching slowly, ice scraping against the hull, chinkling and slurping, another fifty yards to where Harold had fallen in. Still no sign of him. They came to thicker ice, Jake climbed out, tugged on the boat, fell through, and scrambled back in — paddling, swatting, kicking, climbing out, falling through, losing track of the number of times he'd worked his way through the cycle — the distance between him and his son seeming the same, no closer, despite the effort and toil, maneuvering from one soft spot in the ice to the next, one lead to another.

Frank stopped and then Bennie. Jake felt a hand on his shoulder. He continued striking the ice and assaulting it with his feet.

"Jake. Stop," Frank said.

"We've got to get to him. He's there."

"We're there, Jake. It was here. He fell through right in here."

"No. It was further — closer to Harvey's Island."

"No, Jake. I put a range on him when he fell through. It was right in here."

Jake lifted himself and stood on the bow. He searched frantically, trying to see through the murkiness enclosing every piece of ice — down into the dark and cold water, scanning for anything, any sign. There was nothing. The ice gurgled and swished — mocking his agitation, gloating at its conquest.

"Come on Jake. Get down off the bow." Frank guided him to the center of the boat.

"I've got to find him. I can't leave him in this cold river."

"He'll turn up, Jake. The river gives back its dead."

"*Its dead?*" Jake murmured. "He's dead?"

Just the three of them — gray figures besieged by a sea of gray ice and the leafless gray elms and oaks of the surrounding forest.

Jake collapsed onto the center seat, unable to move, his whole insides retching in pain.

"It's okay, Jake." Frank patted his shoulder. "I know it's hard. I lost a son myself. But we have to go now. It's the only way you'll see your way through this."

But at that moment, he didn't want to face this reality. A burning rage surged in his gut as tears swelled in his eyes. He hated this river and its icy grip. But he would beat it. He clinched his hands into fists and pounded the seat of the boat. Somehow he would find a way.

Made in the USA
Middletown, DE
05 July 2020